Taking Care

A Novel Exploring Relationships

Ed N. White

Taking Care

A Novel Exploring Relationships

Addison & Highsmith

Addison & Highsmith Publishers

Las Vegas ◊ Chicago ◊ Palm Beach

Published in the United States of America by
Histria Books
7181 N. Hualapai Way, Ste. 130-86
Las Vegas, NV 89166 USA
HistriaBooks.com

Addison & Highsmith is an imprint of Histria Books. Titles published under the imprints of Histria Books are distributed worldwide.

Library of Congress Control Number: 2023939523

ISBN 978-1-59211-346-0 (hardcover)
ISBN 978-1-59211-353-8 (eBook)

Chapter 1

It was cold and gray outside. My girlfriend of the last three years was leaving for Arizona. She said we had no problems, but her mother was ill, and she needed to visit. I wondered if she would return. We'd had no real issues or arguments, but Marilyn had always been a mystery. She had always kept some things carefully inside.

I carried her bags to the car, placing three of them in the trunk and a small one on the backseat floor. I hung her garment bag from the hook above the rear door. I placed the cat carrier in the front seat, securing the seatbelt through its handle with a click. I watched the cat as she crouched into the corner of her carrier, looking worried. I was sad to see her go.

Marilyn went back into the house for a final check of things. Coming back down the front porch steps, she looked attractive and comfortable in her workout suit with stripes on the legs. She had never said how old she was. Of course, I had never asked, but I would have guessed mid-sixties. A few years younger than me. Although, her petite frame, long brown hair, and contemporary wardrobe helped her look ten years younger.

I waited by her car door, not knowing how we would part and sensing she felt the same because she approached me with a bit of caution. We shook hands. After three years of living together, we shook hands upon saying goodbye.

"Drive safely" were the only words I could find as I closed her door. I pressed my palm against the window. She matched it from the inside the glass with hers, then turned the key and drove away. I kept my hand up until the car was out of sight. I didn't know if she saw that in the mirror.

Three years had ended with a handshake and a wave. She was going to stop and visit an old friend in Pennsylvania. She didn't say whether it was a male or female friend, and I hesitated to ask.

I sat on the step for a while after she left, thinking about us. I wasn't sure how long. Finally, I went inside, and the emptiness closed around me with a thud. It felt like I was living in a hollow log.

I turned on all the lights, the TV, and the kitchen radio; closed my eyes and imagined a gathering of people.

I put the kettle on for tea. "So, what now?" I asked no one in particular as my water boiled. I repeated, louder this time, *"What now?"* That felt better, but I still had no answer.

I sat at the kitchen table with a cup of peppermint tea, trying to think positively. Grabbing a notepad from the counter, I started to scribble a to-do list: *Breakfast,* followed by *Wash Dishes.* Then, I abandoned that idea, balled up the paper, and tried a hook shot to the wastebasket. And missed.

During the past few months, I had occasionally thought about writing. I'd long planned on fiction writing, perhaps even a novel. It wasn't that crazy of an idea. With a degree in English Literature, I had produced a few short stories and the occasional poem that appeared in the "Poet's Corner" of the local newspaper. No big deal, they would publish pages torn out of the phone book.

My original plan had been to become a teacher. However, that plan was sidetracked when I enlisted in the Army following the Vietnam War. My military career was cut short when I fell off a truck during training. My foot was run over, resulting in a medical discharge and a permanent limp.

The faculty rosters had been filled while I was away. Still, I landed a temporary position teaching 7th grade English and helping coach the basketball team at Midland Junior High. My contract ended when the regular teacher returned from maternity leave, so I went to work with my father.

Dad owned a hardware store, Phillips & Son, which was established in 1911 by his father. Dad took over the store in 1951. When Dad suffered a stroke, it became my turn to take over. Without my efforts, the store would have closed.

Tools, nails, seeds, and wheelbarrows consumed my time. To be honest, I probably could have done some writing, too, because we weren't always that busy. But my attempts were half-hearted, and the store took over my life when Dad died. Eventually, I sold the store to a large grocery chain that wanted the property to expand its parking lot. I had a lot of free time and no more excuses not to write, so I decided I should try writing my first novel.

When Mother died, I moved into the house she left me. As I was sorting through her things, I found an old Nunn-Bush shoebox filled with photographs. Some were in good condition, but many were yellowed and curled; pictures of our family from the early twentieth century until perhaps ten years ago. Many were of people I didn't know, but there were plenty of the family as I remembered us: Mom, Dad, me, and a dog named Bucky. My intention was to use these photos to frame a narrative for my novel. I hoped it would work.

When Marilyn first came to live with me, she brought her laptop computer. She had taken a night course at North Shore Tech and was quite adept at using it. She taught me the basics; we didn't have computers when I was in college, so I had never learned to type correctly. I used an old Hermes portable for my assignments, but I preferred a yellow legal pad and felt-tipped pen for creative writing. I loved the connection, the tactility from my fingers through the pen as it lightly rasped the thoughts and words I had imagined in blue ink. But I had to admit; typing was much quicker. Marilyn ended up buying me my very own Dell laptop that Christmas.

To get serious about writing, I needed to create an encouraging writing environment. The den was the perfect room; the desk faced a picture window that overlooked the backyard. The only thing I needed was a proper chair.

I drove my commercial van to the Meadowlands strip mall, which had a Staples store. It was incredible, a collection of stuff ranging from candy to computers. And, of course, a lot of chairs.

"Can I help you find something?"

I turned from the chairs to see a young woman wearing a red Staples sweatshirt. A name tag told me her name was Emma.

"I'm looking for a new desk chair," I said, smiling.

"For your office?" she replied, smiling back more brightly than me. "Or something as a casual chair for reading or TV?"

"I didn't realize people did that," I replied. "I need something to use while writing."

"Are you a writer?" she asked eagerly, leaning toward me.

"Not yet, but I want to be. Will be!" I emphasized my intentions.

"This model would be perfect." She lifted a tag attached to the chair arm to show me that it was rated for 5-8 hours of butt occupancy.

I chuckled and asked, "What happens after that? Does it eject you?" We both laughed at my joke.

"Here's a really great feature," she said as she folded down the arms. "You can recline in this with your laptop on your lap." She was back in sales mode.

"I'll take it, Emma."

Before we got to the check-out, she said, "How are you fixed for paper and ink cartridges?"

I didn't even have a printer, but not wanting to appear too out of touch, I said, "I've been thinking about getting a new printer. What would you suggest?"

"Of course, you want a wireless."

"Absolutely." We crossed the store to the printer display, and I agreed to buy her suggestion without a thought.

"Paper?"

"I probably should get more while I'm here."

The paper selections were overwhelming.

"What have you been using?" She smiled at the question, looking back at me.

I pointed and said, "That one," hoping it was appropriate.

"Good choice, one or two?"

"Two, I plan to be very busy."

"What kind of stuff do you write?"

"Mostly fiction; I'm starting a new book now."

"Alright, what's it about?" she was eager for an answer.

"It's a crime novel."

"Wow!"

At the checkout, she asked, "Do you have a Rewards Card?"

My puzzled expression told her no. "I can set you up with one right now. What's your name… address… phone… email address?"

As I answered her questions, I spotted the candy display behind me. I picked up two boxes of Malted Milk Balls (Marilyn's favorite).

"Will that be all, Mr. Phillips?"

"That'll do it. Thanks, Emma." I pushed one of the candy boxes to her before she could bag it. She looked puzzled. "That's a reward for your excellent service."

"I can't…."

"Why not?"

She looked around and said, "Okay, why not," thanking me with a beautiful smile and crinkly eyes.

I left the store feeling good. Roger from the storeroom was outside with my new chair on a rolling cart. We loaded it in the van's side door, and I gave him five bucks.

On the way home, I stopped at a Subway for a meatball sub and a bag of chips. Then I went into the packy next door for beer.

***

When I got home, I lifted the chair box from the van and managed to get it up the stairs without too much trouble. It wasn't that heavy, even for an old guy like me. When I stripped the cardboard box, I realized that assembly was required. Why had I thought it would emerge whole, like a child from the womb?

To continue the infant metaphor, putting it together was *child's play*. I was pleased that I was beginning to think in literary terms. When it was complete, I wheeled it to the desk, took a seat and positioned my hands on the keyboard. It felt a little low. I lifted the lever, and the seat rose adequately. Next, I folded the chair arms, as Emma had suggested, and placed the laptop on my lap. Just as I pressed the power button, the doorbell rang.

As I approached the front room, I saw a small silhouette behind the curtain. When I opened the door, she was facing the street.

"Emma… Hi." The surprise was evident in my voice.

She turned and reached out with a manila envelope. "Hi, Mr. Phillips, your warranty for your chair. I forgot to give it to you at the store and figured I'd bring it on my way home. I only worked a half day today and live near here."

I was glad she had a lot to say because I was momentarily speechless, only managing a friendly, "Thank you. Would you like a cup of tea?"

She hesitated, then surprised me with, "Why not? I've got some free time."

As she stepped inside, she noticed the chair in the den. "Wow! That looks great."

"Go try it out. I'll put a kettle on." I went into the kitchen, somewhat confused. Did this warranty warrant a personal visit? I took two mugs from the cupboard and several boxes of herbal tea bags.

She entered the kitchen and sat on the edge of a chair, as if ready to bolt. "Take your pick." I motioned toward the tea choices. "Would you like milk or sugar… or honey?" I didn't know why I said that, and I doubted I could find any.

"Honey would be great." *Of course.*

I went through the motions of checking the cupboards. "Looks like I'm all out. I'll put that on my list." I didn't think there had been honey in the house since before Marilyn.

She chose Orange Mango, added two spoons of sugar, and dunked the bag repeatedly before letting it sink to the bottom. Finally, she wrapped the string around the handle.

I chuckled and said, “Well, this is a surprise. It’s amazing what a new chair will bring.” We had a short laugh over my comment.

“Is there a Mrs. Phillips?” she asked.

“No. There is a Marilyn, but she left earlier today, driving to Arizona; her mother is ill. She’s been here for three years. I’ve never been married. Have you?” My anxiety was apparent in my voice.

She snorted into the mug, wiped her face, and said, “Not hardly.” Then she asked, “Is Marilyn coming back?”

“Of course, we have plans for the holidays,” I lied.

We talked a little longer, mostly about the weather and other niceties. She finished her tea and left, just another moment’s diversion in my life now emptied of Marilyn. It had been a pleasant conversation. She was a lovely young woman, and I wished her well.

Chapter 2

After Emma left, I washed out the mugs, set them upside down in the drain rack, and returned to my "office," as I now thought of it. This room now had a purpose. The chair was instantly comfortable as I sank into it. Too comfortable. I'd had little sleep last night before Marilyn's departure hit me like *the old ton of bricks.*

The door between our rooms was always closed, but never locked. Our personal sense of privacy was barrier enough. But last night, as I lay restlessly in my bed, I wished for the comfort of intimacy we sometimes had. She would emerge from her room in her cotton pajamas, a couple of buttons unfastened, smiling coyly as she approached my bed. But not last night. That dream died with the gray dawn.

I could have easily closed my eyes and dozed off in the chair, but I considered that the beginning of a bad habit. The chair was for work, the writing of a novel. I went upstairs to my bedroom for a short nap. As I passed Marilyn's now-empty room, I spied one of her socks under the bed. I fished it out with a rolled-up magazine from the nightstand. It was pink and teal striped; one of her favorites. I thought about keeping it as a *talisman*, but that would have been creepy, more like a fetish. I'd mail it to her when she got to Arizona. That would help keep me fresh in her memory.

I intended to nap for a couple of hours, then get up and go through the "archives," which is what I called my shoebox of photos. Unfortunately, putting on pajamas at 4:05 in the afternoon had not been proper planning. I woke up the following morning at 6:18, went downstairs to have breakfast, and realized the kitchen TV had been on all night. *Oh well.*

It was a lovely day, bright and sunny, nearly cloudless, and a comfortable temperature. I took my cereal out on the back deck and ate with the sun warming my face, planning my literary start. When I returned inside, the TV was showing *Community Cares*. Ms. Sheila Tennet, an administrator from the Waverly Senior Citizen Center, was explaining to the moderator how their old van was having problems. The motor had blown, and they couldn't distribute food to many of their shut-in members. The moderator suggested a GoFundMe page. I had a better idea.

I showered, shaved, and dressed before I called Ms. Tennett. I would have felt uncomfortable calling in my pajamas, although I knew that was foolish.

She had a pleasant voice. "This is Sheila. How may I help you?"

"Hi, this is Dexter Phillips," I said, and told her my plan.

She was silent for a moment, then said, "You aren't kidding me, are you, Mr. Phillips?"

"No, Ms. Tennett, I just need to go out and buy another car this morning, and then I'll bring the van to you. If someone could drive me back to the dealer, that would be great."

"Mr. Phillips, you deliver that van, and I'll carry you on my back if I have to."

We both laughed at that before ending the call.

***

I'd been thinking about buying a car for a while. I'd purchase the Dodge van three years ago while I still had the store; it had a purpose then, but I had no use for it now. So, I consulted Mr. Google and decided on a Ford Taurus SEL. It fit into what I considered my new persona — *author*. I transferred money into my checking account via the wonder of my computer (another cyber skill taught by Marilyn). Then drove to the Ford dealership on Morgan Blvd.

I was quickly approached by a young man with his shirt sleeves rolled up, a loose tie, a big smile, and an extended hand. He offered me coffee and started chattering about the benefits of buying a Ford. I had been in retail for years and had not just fallen off the turnip truck. I accepted his hospitality coffee but already knew what I wanted, the dealer price, and the demands I could make. The only thing left was the choice of color. I decided on Tuxedo Black.

Of course, he had to get his manager's approval. "I've got a guy out front ready to write a check for a Taurus. Here's what he wants to pay."

Salesman and Sales Manager approached me with broad smiles. "Mr. Phillips, Terry tells me you've made an offer on that Taurus (he turned and pointed to the lot). Excellent choice, but I'm afraid we can't accept an offer that low, and..."

Before he said more, I said, "Okay." I put the Styrofoam cup on the salesman's desk and started to leave.

After three steps toward the door, he called after me, "Wait, Mr. Phillips, let me try to rerun those numbers."

I took out my checkbook and said, "Also, I want that Dodge van to be vacuumed, washed, and some tire polish painted on."

While they were getting the car ready and calling the bank to check on the check, I walked down the street to a Dunkin', feeling good. I had noticed a framed photo of two young kids on the salesman's desk, so I bought two gift cards in addition to my coffee and jelly stick.

***

I drove the van to the Waverly Center and was met by Ms. Tennett and several of the staff. I had to pose for pictures for their Facebook page. Sheila thanked me several times, shook my hand, and stepped closer. I thought she might kiss me, but she squeezed my hand again, said "thank you" for the tenth time, and asked a woman named Susan to drive me to the Ford Dealer.

With its high-performance engine, tinted windows, rear spoiler, and moon roof, the Taurus was ridiculously out of character for me. But it was a shitload of fun. So instead of going home, I went up into the hills, around tight curves and long straight roads at speeds far greater than I would have dared in the van.

The instrument display was a mystery; I would need to study that. I imagined Marilyn would have it all figured out in minutes. When I got home and parked in the garage, the car looked lost in the space compared to what the van had gobbled up. There would be much more room for Marilyn's car beside it. I laughed when I imagined what the neighbors would think of my new toy.

At the mailbox, I was delighted to find a postcard from Gettysburg, Pennsylvania.

Hi,

The trip is going well. Cat only got car sick once. Lots of traffic on the Interstates. I will probably be in AZ by the end of next week.

M

Just… *M*. No *miss you, how are you doing, see ya on the flip side*… no fucking nothing.

I sat in a porch chair, slumped forward, elbows on my knees, looking at the card. *M*, that was it. I thought about her trip and the "friend" she would visit in Pennsylvania. To be in Arizona *by the end of next week* sure left a lot of time for a visit to this friend. It was her life; I couldn't intrude. I simply missed her a lot, and my life seemed so empty without her.

I went into the house to finally get started on the archives, but I was attracted to the mantle over the never-used fireplace. Five framed photos sat on it, the only ones we had in the house. One was of my parents on their honeymoon in the Poconos, looking young and free. One of Bucky playing with a ball, and one of Bucky shortly before he died, lying on the couch. I always thought he looked sad in that photo.

There were two pictures of me. In the first one, I was playing basketball. In the next, I was in handcuffs. When Marilyn first came to the house, she was somewhat surprised by that photo. It was a picture taken at a Peace Rally in 1971 and I hadn't done anything wrong, but I was the tallest person there so I figured that's why the cops had chosen me. The photo was taken by a college classmate working for The Observer newspaper. He'd sent me a copy and written on the back with a black Magic Marker: *Public enemy #1 was arrested after a fierce gun battle with the FBI.* My mother was ashamed and didn't like the photo. I thought it was hilarious and felt proud of what I stood for.

I also liked the basketball picture, which was taken during a high school game. I was driving to the basket, ball in my extended right hand, and best I remembered,

I made that shot. At least that's how I wanted to remember it. I did well in high school basketball and earned 2nd team All-State in my junior and senior years. After that, I tried out in college but wasn't good enough to make the university team.

I continued to play in various leagues for years and coached kids' teams. Phillips & Son sponsored teams annually until we closed.

We had a backboard on the garage, and my dad had the driveway repaved and hired a guy to paint the keyhole and foul line. The rim was precisely ten feet, and the net was always intact. We would raise the double garage door in order not to crash into it when driving for a lay-up.

Marilyn was quite excited when I taught her how to shoot a basketball, and we spent hours practicing. Eventually, she had gotten pretty good at shooting from the line. One day, she said, "I can beat you."

"I don't think so," I laughed back.

"What's it worth to you?"

I suggested a sex act.

She stared at me with the ball under her arm and said, "I prefer not."

I laughed and said, "You sound like Bartleby."

"Who?"

"Bartleby, The Scrivener, a book by Herman Melville."

"I thought he only wrote about a whale." Before she retired, Marilyn had been an accountant.

I guessed I thought that was too funny, because I offended her with my laughter. She suddenly winged the ball at my crotch and stormed into the house. That was the type of thing I liked about her and missed so much.

I pulled myself out of my daydream and remembered my plan to work on sorting the photos in the archives. Right after dinner, I told myself, I would start. First, I needed to know how to flatten them; for that, I needed to consult Mr. Google again. Right after dinner.

***

Following my mother's death, I gave most of her furniture to the Salvation Army, including the dining room pieces, which were quite nice and must have been expensive when they were first bought. By removing these, I had created my den-turned-office. That was good, except I had no flat space to sort the photos unless I used the floor. The problem with that was it had become increasingly difficult to get off the floor with my onset of arthritis. I thought there had been too many jump shots pounding my knees in the past.

So, the next best thing came to mind — Marilyn's bed. I took the box upstairs, along with a beer. The curled photos were not going to work for me.

Back downstairs, I asked Mr. Google: *How to uncurl old photos.* He replied in 0.61 seconds with 20,900 results. Far more information than I needed. It seemed relatively easy. I learned it was best done with a steam iron used cautiously with something like butcher paper laid over the photo. I didn't have either, so this would have to wait until tomorrow.

Chapter 3

I awoke with a purpose, eager to get out and buy a steam iron and some butcher paper. Walmart would have the iron. I figured I could find the paper at the small bodega where I shopped for ingredients to put in my Mexican dishes.

It may seem surprising that a sixty-nine-year-old confirmed bachelor could cook various meals, not just franks and beans, but it was easy to learn. I took home ec in high school because our basketball coach was dating the teacher, so we were assured a good grade. I also took a cooking class at North Shore Tech when I was sixty, thinking it would be an excellent place to get a date, but it turned out the women in class were much younger. When it came to cooking variety, I thought *why not*, and I began to watch culinary shows on satellite TV.

"Francisco, *que pasa*?" I always greeted my Latino grocer this way. "I need some butcher paper, maybe about five feet off the roll."

"*Muy loco*, Dex, *muy loco*," he said, while laughing and twirling a finger beside his head. "What for, you gonna butcher a chicken?"

Of course, he was kidding, so I responded, "A cow."

I explained my intent, and he ripped off a five-foot piece, expertly tearing it on the thick blade. As he handed it to me, he spotted the car. "That yours?"

"*Sí.*"

"What's an old fart like you doing with a hot little car like that?"

"Picking up hot little *chicas*," I said as I put twenty bucks in a jar on the counter, contributing to the family of a sick kid.

Next stop, Walmart. Housewares, steam irons. The selection was a little overwhelming. None of the packaging said, *Great for flattening curled photographs*. So, I bought the cheapest one and got out of there as soon as possible. Walmart always depressed me.

The website I chose for instruction had a YouTube video that showed me everything I needed to know in under four minutes. Including that Marilyn's bed was not the proper surface to steam curled photos.

Fortunately, it was lunchtime. I made a sandwich, grabbed a beer, and ate on the back porch. After that, I shot baskets for about twenty minutes. I was on fire, sinking a bunch of shots from three-point land. I was sweaty from all that effort and decided to take a shower before handling the photos.

Refreshed, I took the archives downstairs and laid out the first batch in three rows of four photos on a towel spread on the kitchen table. I covered them with butcher paper and began pressing them with the iron on a low-heat setting. It worked.

It took me one hour and two more beers to create several piles of lovely, flat photos. From the garage, I brought in a piece of plywood and a couple of five-pound barbell discs to place over the images for the night. Tomorrow, the plan would be to identify the people and time frames.

Chapter 4

The next day, it was raining hard. I was sitting in "command central." That's what I called my new chair. Looking out the back window, I noticed the garage door was up. I usually kept it closed this time of year, because raccoons were looking to set up a winter home. I had forgotten yesterday in my haste to flatten photos. No harm, no foul, and I had an excellent view of my new car.

The photo flattening had worked well, except for some of the timeworn photos that were now showing cracks. But these were pictures of people I didn't know or care about anyway.

The family had come here from England in the late nineteenth century following the Industrial Revolution, escaping the farm to emigrate for a "better life." However, anecdotal family history showed it wasn't that much better, because work in the textile and leather mills was challenging and dangerous.

The family history said they struggled in poverty until Great-Grandfather "Willie" Phillips invented a tool used in textile roller printing. After that, life dramatically improved for the Phillips clan. Not too many years later, Phillips & Son Hardware was born. Of course, the Great Depression put a big dent in that, and by the time my father took over, we were down to one store. I had sold that one store on Brady St. for a lot of money several years ago.

I'd never thought much about money. We always seemed to have enough. And with no home mortgage and a hefty bank account, including some managed investment funds, why would I worry? For years following my military accident and medical discharge, I received monthly disability checks. Nothing huge, but several hundred dollars each month that I would stow away in my top desk drawer. Every year, I'd cash out and contribute to a Veteran's cause or organization. It was the least I could do.

Why was I thinking about this? I needed to focus on my book; getting sidetracked was incredibly easy. I decided I was going to make some oatmeal, have another cup of coffee, and get to it. I remembered I also needed to go grocery shopping.

That was something we always did together, Marilyn and me. When she came to live with me, we didn't set up any plan of who did what and when — it just evolved. As an accountant, she took over the finances, writing checks for monthly expenditures on a shared account or paying online with a shared password. She could cook, but she didn't like to. However, she planned the menus. When we shopped on Thursdays, she knew exactly which aisle to go to and it expedited the process, whereas I took forever shopping on my own. She knew wine. I assumed she'd had an active social life, because she had good party instincts. I liked to cook and was good at it. We made a great team.

When I sold the store, I continued to sponsor the bowling team, and that's how I met Marilyn. We rolled in the Wednesday Night Business League along with my three buds. We entered the finals in second place, with an excellent chance of victory.

Marilyn was on the bank team we were competing against. She was a good bowler and, with her handicap, she beat me by eleven pins. Close, but no cigar. That's exactly what she'd said: "Close, but no cigar, Dex." She put a hand on my arm and added, "C'mon, I'll buy the loser a beer." At the bar, we made a date for Saturday. That went well, and I picked her up again Sunday for a ride out to the cape in my van. She got over the initial surprise of the van and drove it on the way home. Two weeks later, she moved in with me.

***

I was accumulating a stash of flattened photos. At first, I thought I'd group them by size, but that didn't make sense. So, I started with the subjects, places, and my best estimate of their age. That worked well for a while. I broke those groups into known and unknown people. I took them upstairs and spread them on Marilyn's bed. I sat on her dressing table bench with a beer, trying to absorb the photographic history before me.

I thought of Marilyn sitting and brushing her hair every morning. I always thought that thing about one hundred strokes was a joke, but she did not. One morning, I interrupted her count to ask a question, and she got pretty pissed at me. I retaliated by saying, "Get a life." That thought brought me a smile.

She was always careful with her makeup, which I assumed was quality stuff. With all those years of office employment, she had developed a technique to always look her best. She always looked good at home, too, while I was more casual about my appearance. Not sloppy, but casual.

We kept the house in the same manner as the cooking and groceries: the duties just evolved. She did the laundry, including ironing when needed, and dusting. I did the vacuuming, the bathrooms, and the dishes, which were no big deal with the dishwasher.

I enjoyed mowing the lawn, but when Francisco told me he had a nephew that did lawns and could use the money for school, I gave him the job. He did well, and I paid him more than he asked. I let him use the mower to do another lawn down the street too. Good kid; I knew he would do well.

Last night, I began grouping my family pictures. Most of these did not need to be steamed. I started to sort them into Mother and Father with me; Mother and Father alone; me alone; me with the dog. Indoors, outdoors, and a miscellaneous category because I was getting tired of this shit. I went back downstairs for another beer and some baseball.

With the Red Sox leading by six runs in the bottom of the fifth inning, it was easy to fall asleep on the couch. I was awakened by my cell phone as it sounded the refrain from *Oh, Susannah.* Marilyn had done that for me. The screen said *MARILYN.*

I said, "Hi," Trying to wake up fast.

"Hi, back at ya." She replied brightly. This would be a good conversation.

"How's your trip going?"

"I'm still in Pennsylvania."

"Oh… how's the cat?"

"She's good; I taught her how to walk with a Flexi-lead, so we've been doing that several times a day. Unfortunately, there's too much traffic to let her loose."

"How's your friend?"

"Sleeping."

"And your mom?"

"My sister says she's stable right now, but…"

"I didn't know you had a sister?"

"I have two."

With that surprising news, I stopped talking for a moment, trying to think of something more. "I bought a new car."

"Really, what kind?" She seemed genuinely interested.

"Ford, Taurus SEL… Tuxedo Black."

"Wow! That's a little out of your comfort zone, isn't it?"

"Maybe, but wait 'till you see it… and there's a lot more room in the garage for you."

"Dex, I've gotta go. I'll call you next week." She cut the call, and I sat there thinking with the phone still pressed to my ear. What was she trying to tell me?

Unpleasant thoughts were bouncing around in my head when my cell lit up again: TOM B. "Tomeee, what's up?"

"Charlie and I are at the alleys. Bowling, beers… and maybe babes."

"In your dreams. You guys gonna be there a while?"

"Shit yeah, the league starts in two weeks. So, we need the practice, and that includes you."

"Yeah, yeah, I'll come down and kick your ass."

Over the bowling years, I had accumulated a collection of bowling shirts and jackets. I stayed in my Red Sox t-shirt, but added a Manton All-Stars jacket with *Dex, Hi Game 1998,* embroidered on the left sleeve.

Charlie and Tom were warming up in alley four when I got there. We agreed on five-dollar bets for most strikes, high game, and 7-10 splits made. I was having a good night. In the fourth frame of our third string, Tom asked, "How's Marilyn?" and my game turned to shit.

"She's on her way to Arizona, her mother's sick."

Tom said, "So, it's just you and the cat."

"The cat's with her."

Charlie leaned toward me and said, "She's probably not coming back." I ignored him and studied the score projected on the screen over the alley. By the time we finished, I had lost fifteen bucks.

At the bar, Charlie, the winner, bought the first round. "Jen, give these losers a drink, and how 'bout a kiss for the winner?"

"In your dreams, Charlie." That was the second time I'd heard that tonight. Jennifer was probably in her early thirties, beautiful, and recently divorced. Way out of our league.

Tom started, "So, Marilyn left?"

"She's visiting her sick mother. Don't be an asshole."

Then Charlie asked, "Did she take all her clothes?"

"Of course, she took her clothes; she'll be there a while."

Charlie laughed, "The clothes, the cat… she's not coming back."

"Fuck you guys. Let's talk about something else." I started draining my beer.

"How 'bout, Celia?" Tom leaned a little closer as if to impart some secret.

"Jesus, Tom, I've known your sister for what… fifty years. That would be like dating my own sister."

"You don't have a sister." Charlie jumped in.

"No, shit! Drink your beer. Let's talk about something else."

Tom wouldn't quit. "It's been two years since Ronnie died, Dex. It would be good to get Celia out, just a dinner or something."

"I'll think about it." I emptied my glass and got up to leave, putting a twenty on the bar. "Jen, give my former friends a drink and keep the rest for yourself."

"Thanks, Dex. Take care."

Tom turned on his stool and asked, "Why so early?"

"I've got a big day tomorrow."

Charlie looked up and said, "Doing fuck what?"

"I'm writing a book." As soon as I said that, I wished I hadn't.

"A book! You've gotta be shittin' me." Charlie was always expressive.

I kept walking toward the door, calling back, "Let's do this again next week. You guys need more practice."

Tom said, "Take care, Dex; we'll see you."

I was in the parking lot, unlocking the door before I realized I'd forgotten to tell them about my new car.

Chapter 5

In the morning, right after breakfast, I intended to finish the photo steaming, categorize the photos, and get started on an outline if there were no further interruptions. Breakfast went well; it was hard to screw up oatmeal.

I had lumped many of the old photos in a category I called "early history." The picture that stood out was of a young boy, perhaps eight or ten years old. He was standing at attention with a toy gun on his shoulder. I assumed it was my paternal grandfather, who volunteered as an ambulance driver in France in 1918 during the "War to End All Wars." *Yeah, right.* I was too young to pay attention to many of the stories he told. But now, I wondered if he had met Hemingway, John Dos Passos, E.E. Cummings, or any of the other great writers who had also volunteered. It made me curious whether I had some literary heritage, even though it would be secondhand at best.

I was only five when he retired from the store and told the family he wanted to tour the old battlefields before he died. However, he visited the historic sites *and* died. His heart stopped beating while viewing the monument to the Ypres campaign in Belgium after spending six days with a tour group. He was cremated there, and his ashes were returned to my father via airmail.

The more I dug into the archives, the more fascinating it became. I had planned to put notes on file cards to have a loose outline, but I had no cards. I thought I did, but they had been filled with recipes, both sides, that my mother had written in her left-leaning, precise script.

I could go to Staples, but I didn't want to run into Emma and have her question my progress. So, I cut some copy paper in half, which worked just fine. The writing of information on my makeshift cards was a different story. I got up for more coffee and checked the freezer for the supply of ready-made meals. Marilyn had insisted I get them because I would be *discombobulated* for a few days after she left and not want to cook. For God's sake, that was a word my mother occasionally used. I thought about going outside and shooting hoops.

Instead, I sat down with the coffee, took out my cell, checked the time, and figured, *what the hell.* I called Celia Frank, Tom Brandt's sister.

When she answered, I put on my brightest voice. "Hi, Celia, Dex Phillips. I hope I'm not calling too early."

"Dex, so good to hear from you. Early? Not at all; I just got back from a run."

"Wow! That's good to hear… so you're doing okay?"

Her response seemed to stiffen, "Why wouldn't I be?"

"No reason. I just thought I'd call; we haven't talked since the funeral."

"Did Tommy tell you to call?"

"What? No, I…"

"Dex, don't lie to me. I've known you for what? Fifty years? … Was it Tom?"

"Maybe."

"He's a pain in the ass. You know Ronnie died two years ago doing what Ronnie did best — being a reckless fool. You don't go out in a goddamn electrical storm to climb on the roof with a metal ladder."

"I guess not."

"Dex, I loved him, and he was very good to us… but it's over. We've moved on. Jill has a good job and is getting married next month. Ronnie, Junior is starting med school, and we're doing just fine, Dex… we're doing fine. For some reason, Tommy thinks I need to go out with a guy, have dinner with a guy, jump in bed with a guy. Screw that. I don't need any of it. We're doing just fine."

It sounded like her voice was beginning to crack, and I had an image of a tear-stained face. "Well, I just thought I'd call. It sounds like everything is fine… my number is on your screen. Put me in your contacts just in case… maybe we can have coffee sometime."

"Maybe we can… how's Marilyn?"

"She's good… coffee sometime, the three of us, Cel'… the three of us."

"See ya, Dex. Take care."

***

That thing with the note file outline didn't end up working so well. I decided on a short, handwritten scenario as the ideas came into my head — a kind of "stream of consciousness" outline system. I felt more comfortable with that than starting directly on the laptop.

I found the bulk of the chair kept me a little too far away from the desk surface to be comfortable, so I grabbed a small pillow off the couch as lumbar support. While I was up, another coffee was a good idea, and I got the mail I had forgotten since Wednesday. Just a bunch of shit, no postcard, but there was a bill from the gas company.

This pushed me in a new direction. Since Marilyn used to handle our finances, this would again be my responsibility, at least for the short term. I didn't want to appear stupid about this. I had lived for many years before her, writing checks and paying my bills on time. The difference was now, many of these bills were paid online.

When Marilyn explained all this, I only half-listened, thinking, *so?* Well, *so* had become *now*.

Good old Marilyn had put all the accounts and passwords in a small, spiral-bound notebook with a floral design on the cover. I remembered she'd stored it in the top right-hand drawer. A piece of cake. I'd log on and pay the gas bill right after lunch.

Right now, I wanted to get started on my "life vignettes," as I had come to think of them. I wanted to take something easy out of the archives, so I chose a picture of me with a new bicycle and the dog in the background.

THE BICYCLE

I remember this very well. It was a Monarch, blue with white stripes. A tapered "tank" ran from the seat to the handlebar stem. It had a compartment for the batteries that powered the headlight and horn. The horn button was on the right side of the tank. It had one set of sprockets and large balloon tires, giving it a smooth ride. I had attached two playing cards onto the fender supports with a spring-loaded clothespin. These cards brushed against the spokes as I pedaled, making a staccato sound that, in my mind, was a motor. I'm sure it made the bike faster, especially in the dark. The handgrips had multi-colored streamers, and the seat had a sheepskin cover. There was a red reflector on the back fender. I got it for my tenth birthday. Somehow, Dad had hidden it in the garage and then gotten up early on the morning of my birthday to set it on the back porch.

A year later, I had stripped the fenders, tank, and chain guard, turned the handlebars to face forward, and removed the streamers. Then, I raced around the neighborhood with my friends on similar stripped-down "hotrods," laying them in the dirt when we stopped because we also had removed the kickstands.

I read this several times, thinking, *not bad*, and was suddenly aware of the effort it had taken to go into my past. I felt exhausted. I didn't expect to feel so much emotion as I sifted through my life. I wasn't sure I liked it, and thought maybe I needed to ease into this; use photos of other people and places that did not have such an effect, then work back into my personal life slowly.

I called Tom Brandt to see if he wanted to hit a bucket of balls at the driving range.

Chapter 6

Tommy and I were like brothers from different mothers. We grew up together, spending equal time in each other's houses. Our parents were close friends, so it was natural we would also be. I had no siblings, but Tom had a sister four years younger than us, so she rarely entered the picture of our youthful activities. Our closest buddies growing up were Charlie Osbourne and Dick Lane. The four of us were inseparable from our early school days through Scouts, sports, rowdy behavior, and teenage girlfriends. At the end of high school, three of us went to college. Charlie went to work for the electric company, eventually becoming a field superintendent.

Charlie's problem was booze. He drank through two marriages, although he remained good friends with both women, even today. My parents called Charlie "a good egg." He was funny, never ugly or violent, merely irresponsible. I thought both those women — and I knew them well — still had feelings for him. He had two sons with his first wife, both of whom were married and doing well with their own families.

Barbara and I never had children. We tried a lot, but it never happened for us. We had one consultation with a fertility doctor, but decided not to get tested. We thought too much of each other to assign blame. We thought about adoption and somewhat selfishly decided we did not want to share our relationship with someone else. Not that it would matter; we were torn apart by her tragic death thirty-seven years ago. When asked by someone I didn't know very well, I found it easier to say I was never married.

I met Tom at the Mountainview Driving Range. I never understood the name because there were no mountains in sight, probably just an owner with an overactive imagination. Tom was a helluva good golfer, not quite pro, but damn close. Having sold a profitable business and retired at age sixty, he played a lot of golf. His handicap was consistently in the low single digits when we played in leagues.

Like me, he had been married but had no children. After twenty-eight years of marriage, his wife met a guy in an online chat room and moved to Oregon. I think Tom handled it well and moved on; he was presently dating a woman from Somerset, Massachusetts. I'd met her a few times, and she seemed nice. We had a quick beer after hitting balls, but I needed to get home and get started on the book.

Tom liked my new car. "Pretty sporty for an old dude," was his comment as we shook hands and parted.

I thought about Dick Lane, the smart one, on the drive home. Dick went to med school and became an ophthalmologist. We called him "Dick Doc." He was a charming guy who had been donating his time in clinics all over the state since his retirement four years ago. He was the good one, married all these years to the same woman who had emigrated from Vietnam with her family after the war. They had one child, now a beautiful woman and also an ophthalmologist, who took over her father's practice.

At home, I checked the mail, just in case, and made a sandwich of lunch meat, cheese, and mayo on one slice and grape jelly on the other. Why not? The beer went well with this combination.

***

My cell announced a call just as I was dozing off on the couch: *MARILYN.* I thought, maybe this was the formula: lie down on the couch, fall asleep, and she will call.

I shook my head to clear it for speech and croaked out a, "Hey."

"Hey, back at ya."

"You sound pretty chipper today."

"I am. I'm leaving tomorrow; Phil doesn't need me anymore."

"Phil?"

"Phyllis Lohner; she's a well-known ceramic artist; she signs all her work P-H-I-L. She's having a big showing at a regional craft fair, and I was helping her get ready. Unfortunately, her wife is temporarily away."

"Wife?"

"Phil's gay, a lesbian. Her wife, Vivian, is a vascular surgeon doing a semester teaching gig at Penn State's med school."

"Wow! I don't know what to say."

"Don't say anything, Dex. You're not concerned, are you?"

"Of course not."

"We've been together long enough… you wouldn't have concerns?"

"Of course not… how's the cat?"

"She's great; you should see her."

"I'd like to…."

"We'll see, Dex, we'll see. I've gotta go."

She ended the call, and the same shit hit me as with the last call. I just sat there with the phone in my hand, not knowing what to do next. At least the "mystery friend" mystery was solved, I thought. But the feeling in the pit of my stomach was still there — I missed Marilyn.

***

This was a relatively large house, built in the mid-twenties. There were both front and rear stairs to the second floor. When I was stressed out, I would climb the front stairs, traverse the corridor, head down the back stairs through the kitchen, and repeat. Sometimes I would reverse the order. I found this an easy way to reduce my stress and reorder my thoughts. I did this now. After three trips, I had settled enough to go to my office, slump in the chair, and stare at the archives.

In the box were many similarly sized photos, probably taken from the same camera. Some of these had names and dates written on the back. Most of the details were in my mother's distinctive handwriting. I was aligning the edges of a bunch of them like a deck of playing cards when one dropped in my lap. It was me with a fishing rod. I loved fishing, but then I'd had a couple of bad experiences.

I didn't like to think of this, but knew it would probably work well in the book. I made a few outline notes and then began typing on my keyboard.

THE FISH

Dad bought me a Zebco spinning rod and reel for my thirteenth birthday. This was a huge step up from the old level-wind that had been his. I spent hours casting a small lead weight, trying to land it in an empty bucket set in the back yard. I got pretty good at it.

I stopped for a minute, tried to relax, then continued

There was a man, I won't give his name. I'll call him Mr. W, whose son was part of our scout troop. He offered to let us come to his house and fish in his stocked trout pond. Mr. W was wealthy; the house was large, on a hill with a sloping lawn to the pond. It was an artificial pond created merely for his use and heavily stocked with trout. The size to a thirteen-year-old seemed more extensive than it was, but it had to be at least 200 feet across, with a dam on one end with a pipe spillway. There was a screened intake from a slowly flowing stream on the other end. Us scouts were circled around the edge near the stream. I had my new rig, a small metal tackle box lying open, and a cardboard box of worms. The store where my dad bought the new rod and reel was having a fishing contest: the largest trout would win a nice prize.

Mr. W came from the house, fully equipped. He had more fishing stuff than I had ever seen in one place. He stayed away from us and began long looping casts with his fly rod, dropping the tiniest hooked thing out in the pond without a splash. I put a worm on the hook and a bobber on the line and cast it as best I could.

It wasn't long before I had a strike and started yelling and reeling, pulling a large brown trout out of the water to flop at my feet. Mr. W. put down his rod and came running, saw the fish, saw the knife in my tackle box, and said something like, "We need to gut it now!" Then, in a jealous rage, he cut the head and tail off the fish, slashed its belly, and let the guts spill on the grass. I pulled my hat down and walked away so no one would see me crying.

Sonofabitch! When I read this now, I still got tears in my eyes. But I wasn't done with this guy yet. I printed that story and then started on:

THE BOAT

Besides the big house with the trout pond, Mr. W also had a second home on a lake in Vermont. Later that summer, the troop was invited to camp for a weekend. Mr. W had his own beach, dock, and diving float. He had a speedboat and a small wooden rowboat. We went up there in three cars on a Friday afternoon. Tom, Charlie, Dickie, and I traveled with Dickie's father.

We pitched tents, went swimming, and jumped off the float. Made a fire ring and cooked hotdogs and marshmallows over the coals. Mr. Marchetti, one of the other fathers, told ghost stories when it got dark. It was the best camping experience I have ever had.

After breakfast, some kids went into town on Saturday morning with Mr. Marchetti and Mr. Lane. Tom, Charlie, and I stayed behind with Mr. W's son to do more fishing. I'll just call him J. He suggested we take the rowboat to deeper water to try for bigger fish.

We were all good swimmers and had flotation seat cushions. Everything was going well, but the wind had shifted and got stronger, so rowing was difficult. Tom and I were in the middle seat, each pulling an oar but not pulling well together, so we started drifting toward a point of land. As we got closer and into the lee, we could pole the boat in the shallows close enough to jump out and pull it along with the bowline back toward camp.

We were laughing, splashing, and kidding around when Mr. W crashed through the shoreline brush, scaring the living shit out of us. He waded into the water, grabbed his kid by the neck, and pushed his head under the water. Charlie threw a rock at him, and we ran toward camp, terrified and screaming, scratching our way through the brush, hearing J's screams for help and Mr. W blasting him with swear words.

Mr. Lane had just gotten back in camp when he heard our cries and ran toward us. When we saw him coming through the brush, we tried to tell him what had happened but couldn't get the words out. We all just pointed, and he kept running toward the commotion.

When we returned to camp, Mr. Marchetti was there to calm the other kids, not knowing what had happened. We were gasping and scared and scratched from the brush, blood showing on our arms and legs.

Mr. Lane returned with his arm around J, who was crying his eyes out. Mr. W was nowhere in sight. The two parents went off by themselves, whispering. They came back, told us to pack our gear, and that they would drive us home.

I never saw Mr. W again but kept thinking, when I was older, I'd confront him about this. J never told anyone what happened after we left the boat. About three months later, Mr. W hanged himself in the garage while J was at school. The family moved elsewhere as soon as they could sell the house.

This took a lot out of me. I settled back in the chair and realized I was short of breath and my heart was doing a rapid dance. I was stressed to the max. Fifty-six goddamn years, and that sonofabitch still haunted me. I didn't like the word "hate," but that's how I thought of the man. It was time to move on.

I needed some better thoughts, so I stared out the window, overlooking the porch, and thought of Marilyn. I felt her last call had some promise; *We'll see, Dex, we'll see.*

We had two chaise lounges on the porch and had spent many quiet evenings having wine and honest conversations. Before she left, we were thinking about putting a hot tub outside. Although we were kind of old, we were both in pretty good shape; I had been slim my whole life, and Marilyn worked hard at keeping a younger-looking body. We joked a little about being naked in the tub after dark, but I'm sure that's what we would have done.

The weather was changing as we got out of summer and into fall. I remembered the old Dylan lyrics from *Subterranean Homesick Blues.* I loved that song from the anti-war days. I didn't need a weatherman to tell me that rain was coming; my ankle was beginning to hurt. Since my military accident, I had been a little gimpy on that leg. I was adept at wrapping it with an ACE bandage before playing golf, shooting hoops, or even mowing the lawn. I had to wear a custom orthotic in that shoe to compensate for the misaligned foot — no big deal.

I remembered the old line; *I cried because I had no shoes, then I met a man with no feet.* I liked the Blues Brothers' adaptation better; *I cried because I had no shoes, then I met a man who had no class.* I had to laugh at that again and felt better for it. Shit, I wished Marilyn would come home.

Chapter 7

I did pretty much nothing on the book over the weekend. Steamed a few more old pictures without learning anything new. I wrote another outline for a piece entitled *THE COAT*, trying for something with a bit of humor. I wasn't at my best between *THE FISH, THE BOAT,* and Marilyn. Monday morning was an anniversary — one week since Marilyn had left.

I was trying to decide on a mood for the day when I had an incoming call from *CHARLIE.*

"Chuck, how ya doing?"

"Okay. Dex, but I need a ride… if you can. I get my license back in ten days."

"The next time you're stopped, they're gonna shoot first and breathalyze later."

"Very fucking funny… I have a doctor's appointment… Tom's out of town, and my boys are at work."

"Hey, no problem, Chuck, just yankin' you a little. Who're you going to see?"

"An entomologist."

"That's a guy who studies bugs."

"Whatever, this asshole wants to put a pipe down my throat to check my stomach."

"What's been happening?"

"Stomach problems for about two months. Going off and on."

"And you drink and drink."

"Don't fuck with me."

"Sorry, man, bad joke, sure I'll take you. What time?"

"The appointment is at ten thirty, Southside Medical.

"I'll pick you up at ten. Sorry for the bad joke."

"No problem, I deserved it."

"Take care."

***

Charlie Osbourne was an enigma. He drank a lot of booze and, oftentimes, couldn't remember where he parked his car, but his condo at Westwood was always neat and orderly, as was he. I couldn't recall ever seeing him unshaved, although the styptic-covered scars sometimes displayed a rough start. When he drove drunk, he drove slowly. The more intoxicated, the slower, and one time was arrested for parking in the middle of the road. Of course, this was dangerous behavior, and this last episode resulted in a one-year loss of license, which, apparently, was nearly over. All of us shared the load, transporting him as necessary.

Charlie's call took me away from the book and the Marilyn problems, but I didn't like the sound of his medical condition.

He was waiting out front of his condo when I pulled up. He spread his arms, palms up, and said, "What the fuck… what pimp did you steal this thing from?"

"Get in; we're running late." No other words were said on the way.

I let him out at the main entrance, "Call me when you're done."

I parked and began reading a Charles Todd novel. The authors were a mother and son writing team with stories featuring either a Scotland yard inspector or a nursing sister set during WWI in England and France. But, again, I thought about my grandad.

***

After he called, it took a few minutes to get from the parking garage to Charlie. It took me longer than that to get over his appearance. He looked like he had aged ten years in the past hour. His usually-flush complexion was now gray and drawn. He was standing at the curb, looking down at his shoes.

When he got in the car, I saw his eyes were red-ringed. I was sure he had received bad news.

"So," I tried to sound upbeat. "What did the asshole tell you?"

It took him a minute to answer, and his voice was subdued. "More tests," he said. "I need some more tests, and they scheduled me for tomorrow. He said I might be here for a few hours because of something... I didn't understand it all."

"I'll take you. What time?"

"I can probably get one of my boys..."

"I'll drive you," I said more forcefully, unable to hide my concern.

"Thanks, Dex; I have to be there at seven. I can't eat tonight after ten. Fuck!"

I offered to buy lunch, or at least stop for a coffee, but he wanted to go right home, saying he was tired. This man was not the Charlie Osbourne I had known for many years.

***

Tuesday morning. It was almost two hours before Charlie called from the hospital. I had finished the Todd novel and rested my head against the seat. I wasn't sure how to read him when he got in the car. He looked brighter than the day before.

"Well. I've got it."

"Got what?" I asked, looking skeptical and alarmed.

"A big motherfucking tumor on my liver."

I didn't know how to respond, so I asked, "Is that what they told you?"

"They didn't say motherfucking."

"Oh, Jesus God." I undid my seatbelt and turned to him, grasping his arm. "Oh, Jesus, Charlie... Charlie... oh, shit!" I was the one who fell apart. "What's next?"

"Let's get a drink."

"I mean, with the doctors?"

As I drove away, heading toward the nearest decent bar, he told me of the plan to start an aggressive chemo protocol immediately. "I told them I'd try it, and if I don't like it — *no mas.*"

"Holy shit! What did they say?"

"Doctor stuff, I don't know, Dex. My grandmother went through this shit, and all it did was stall for time, and she went through hell. I'm not gonna do that."

I had no response.

When we settled into the bar at O'Malley's Irish Pub, he gave me more details. The tumor was extensive; he forgot how many centimeters, and it was inoperable. With aggressive treatment, they expected he could live another nine months.

"I'm gonna give it one shot, Dex. I'm curious to try, but I'm not gonna prolong this thing."

I had no answer.

We each had another round, but his face began to show discomfort. I drove him home, only saying I'd pick him up in the morning. As I drove away, I pounded the steering wheel, "Shit! Shit! Shit!"

***

When I got home, a letter from *M. Brewer* was in the mailbox. I sat on a porch step to read:

Hi Dex,

I'm writing because I can't trust my voice on a call. So, the doctors have moved Mom to a hospice. It was a tough decision for my sisters and me, but it was best for Mom. She's reached a point where the only thing left is to make her comfortable. They think she only has a few days. I will be here after she passes, with the funeral and to settle her estate. Then, I think I'm coming home.

The cat sends her love. She's lying in my lap, purring, as I write this.

As ever,

M

I wasn't sure I was awake. Was this some dream that might pass in the morning? Charlie… Marilyn… her mother. It was a lot to process. My brain was chattering. I reread it… *I think I'm coming home.* Of course, she means here. It was the vague,

I think, part that bothered me. I'm glad the cat loved me. I wish Marilyn had said the same. *As ever,* I'd settle for another three years.

It took a while to unwind. I was hungry after the two drinks and needed something to smooth out my stomach. I made oatmeal. I also decided to sign up for an email account, thinking I could get longer responses from Marilyn through that medium.

Chapter 8

I reread *THE COAT*. It wasn't all that funny.

THE COAT

My Mother was an RN, although she only worked full-time until she became pregnant with me. I imagine she was an excellent nurse. She often worked part-time as I was growing up. It seemed she never wanted to entirely give up her profession.

All the boys in our community had hooded winter jackets with a center zipper on the hood, and it could be undone to lay flat across the shoulders. I'm not sure what she had against that, but it had something to do with her medical background and exposing the neck to the winter cold. However, she was determined that I not suffer that fate and bought me a coat with a fixed hood, a rounded shape and a drawstring, so it looked like a baby bonnet. As if that were not bad enough, the coat also had a sewn-on belt.

So, all my "gang" had solid color Melton wool jackets in blue, maroon, or green with a zipper hood that was sharply shaped. And here comes "Nancy Boy" with the brown baby bonnet and sewn-in belt. I had several encounters with this. But that's not the bad news.

One cold morning, I was running late. I grabbed my coat off a hanger in the front hall closet, and ran to school just as the morning late bell sounded. I made it to the classroom and whipped off the coat to hang it in the classroom wall's wardrobes. I got to my seat just as the teacher called the roll and realized that my father's shiny brown suit vest was hanging off my skinny shoulders. It had been lurking on the same closet hanger underneath my coat.

That's not funny, but it was devastating as a twelve-year-old. The picture that inspired this story was of me wearing the coat, standing on a large snowdrift in front of our house. My dog was barking on the sidewalk because he couldn't climb the pile. Clearly shown on my feet were galoshes.

If any Gypsies had come through the neighborhood, I would have gladly run off with them. My mother also had a thing about feet, footwear, and growing boys.

Galoshes were just one part of that. I didn't think it was necessary to set up a new outline for this, so I just continued without another title.

All my friends had four-buckle overshoes, which they often left undone, preferring to walk with the flaps open. Mother thought those buckles could do something terrible to my feet, so I had galoshes you step into, then fold over the front and secure with a single strap at the top. Lovely.

The only shoes I wore until I was fourteen were official Boy Scout shoes, moccasin toe, low leather brogues. Most kids wore sneakers, but in Mother's view, these did not provide adequate support. That was her theory. I bought my own Converse All-Stars with the money I made on my paper route.

As the weather got colder, many kids wore high-tops, lace-up leather boots with a snap-closing pocketknife pouch on the outside of the right boot. I don't have to tell you what she thought about that.

I didn't know where these stories are going, but I did something literary today. I thought about calling Dick Doc and discussing Charlie's situation. But that was Chuck's private matter, not for me to blab about. He'd tell Tom and Dick in his own way.

***

I went grocery shopping. Anything to fill the time before tomorrow morning. It was time to replenish my cooking larder since I was sure I was no longer *discombobulated*. I needed to tell Marilyn that. Pushing the cart down aisle four, going for some dry black beans, I heard a young voice say, "Mr. Phillips."

I turned to see Emma walking toward me: beautiful smile on her face; basket in her hands. "Hi, Emma, what a surprise."

"I told you I lived in this neighborhood." Her teeth were very white.

"You did; I remember that now. How's everything?"

"Excellent. I don't work at Staples anymore."

"Oh."

"Yeah, I'm at Dunkin' now. I'm going to be *Assistant Night Manager* in three months. So, stop in and see me."

I went on high alert. The last thing I needed right now was an overfriendly young woman barely out of her teens. "I will. Right now, I've got to get home. I have guests coming for dinner. Good luck with your new job."

"Thanks, Mr. Phillips, and you take care."

Sonofabitch, the first thing I did when I got home was look in the hall mirror. Was I really someone who looked like they needed to "take care?"

After putting the groceries away, I thought about calling Marilyn. But she never answered her phone and always let it go to voicemail, which pissed me off. Texting also pissed me off because I was not very adept at it. I thought about trying my couch nap theory to attract her call, but that was just being stupid. *What the hell,* I thought. *I'll call and leave a message.*

"Hey, so sorry to hear about your mom. It's easy to offer help from a distance, but I really mean it. I'll be glad to fly down there if you want me to. Really, it would be no problem. I've never been to Arizona. Think about it. I can meet your sisters, too. And my condolences to them, also. And the cat, tell her I miss her, too. I'm cooking dinner now. I wish you were here."

I cut the call before I could sound any more stupid. I'd been speaking fast, uncomfortable with what I was saying. Still, I had meant it. I'd fly down there in a heartbeat. I really did miss Marilyn.

There was a little time before dark to shoot some hoops. I had lights out there, but lately, they'd affected my shooting. I had glaucoma, and I thought maybe it was getting a little worse. The rings around the lights were beginning to look like the rings of Saturn. Perhaps it hadn't been a good idea to stop taking the drops after the last laser session. I should have told Dick Doc I had stopped; maybe he would have encouraged me to finish the prescription.

There was always a Plan B for how to spend my time. First, I would work on the book. I thought it was time to introduce Bucky. I'm not sure why had I named him that; I was only about six years old when he came into our lives. This was going to be a tough one to write. I could feel it in my bones.

THE DOG

It was winter; I remember that much. We were returning from a Sunday afternoon visit to family friends. Dad let us out at the front door and put the car away in the garage. The porch light had been burned out for a while, and it was dark in the shadows. Mother put the key in the lock, pushed open the door, and screamed as some animal ran past her, into the house. I jumped back, too scared to speak. She reached around the door frame and hit the hallway light switch as Dad came running from the backyard.

At the end of the hall, by the kitchen, was a dog — small, scruffy, waggy, mouth open, panting. His ears were up, his body shaking, looking like he wanted to play.

Dad said, "Wait out here, don't go near him." He went to the back porch and opened that door, reaching in for the kitchen switches and the porch light, holding the door open so the dog would go out. He didn't; he flopped on his back, tongue hanging out, pulsing, doing an upside-down dog dance on the linoleum floor. Dad went in, knelt, scratched his stomach, and the dog went into overdrive with the back legs moving to a faster beat.

Mom called from the front door, even though she could see the ferocious beast on the floor, "Is it okay?" Dad just started laughing, and I was half-way to the kitchen floor before he could answer. I don't think there was a happier dog on the planet.

He had no collar or tag. He was thin, and his coat looked like he had been living rough for a while. His nails were very long, and some were cracked. But his eyes were bright, and he didn't look sick or injured. "Can we keep him… can we keep him, Dad… Mom… please, can we keep him."

Sometimes parents have a way of communicating in the presence of their children that says everything without using words. They looked at the dog and at each other.

"Can we keep him, please, please?"

Monday morning, Dad went to a pet store and bought a collar, leash, dishes, dog food, brushes, nail clippers, and toys. So I guess that was the answer. Next, he called

Animal Control and cryptically asked about missing dogs, not saying we had found one. Then, satisfied that he was not some other poor kid's lost pet, he asked me, "What's his name?"

"Bucky," I said. I don't know why I called him that. Did it matter?

I liked this part of the story and reread it. But then, I decided to continue, against my better judgment.

To say Bucky was part of the family was an understatement. Where we went, he went. My mother made a cover for the back seat of the Oldsmobile to handle the loose fur. He spent part of the time with his head in my lap being petted or with his head out the window, ears back, mouth open, tongue flapping, getting high on the turbo scents driven into his nose. Dad hired some guys to put a fence around the backyard so we could just open the back door, and Bucky had a kingdom of his own. Shade, trees, squirrels, and a growing boy to act foolishly with.

Of course, as this boy got older, the contact became less and less and settled into morning and evening petting and some kind words. Then, finally, dad began to pick up the slack. He enjoyed taking Bucky for evening walks and smoothing the scraggly coat as the dog lay beside his recliner and watched TV.

All good things must come to an end, and for dogs, that's not a long time. I was old enough to drive when Bucky began to falter. He loved to ride with me, jumping up on the seat, putting his paws on the passenger door armrest, and sticking that quivering nose into the moving air. It wasn't long before I had to lift him up to the seat, and he just lay there with his nose touching my leg. One morning he didn't get out of his little dog bed and just kept sleeping.

Dad was away at a hardware trade show, so Mom and I buried him in the backyard under a blue spruce. I dug the hole, and Mom wrapped him in an old flannel sheet. When I had finished tamping the dirt in place, I turned to my mother, and uncontrollable tears burst from my eyes. That's all I'm going to say.

Chapter 9

Well, I messed myself up plenty good last night. Between the dog narrative, Charlie thoughts, too much Vodka, and missing Marilyn, I had a crappy, restless sleep. When the digital clock read 2:15 a.m., I figured I had better set the alarm, something I rarely did. Three hours later, waking long before the alarm went off, I lay on my back, stuffed another pillow under my head, and tried to make sense of this turmoil. I was confronted with images of my long-deceased wife, Barbara. Not something I wanted to talk or think about, but this morning, I couldn't escape.

Pictures of her flooded my brain: good times, bad times, death. I sat at her side in Hospice, unaware if she could hear me as I read to her. Barbara was also a teacher, except she had a real job teaching high school English for seven years. This included the year in which she tried so hard, despite the devastating headaches that sometimes caused her to scream in pain at home. Even though she could not complete that final semester, she was awarded "Teacher of the Year." It wasn't a sympathy vote. She was that good and she deserved it. The funeral was small. We weren't a large family. We maintained a close circle of friends, but the memorial celebration for her at the high school packed the gym.

That was the only time I ever took a tranquilizer. I didn't think I'd have been able to function without it. My mother called the doctor, and we stopped at the pharmacy on our way to the service. She returned to the car with a glass of water and an envelope with six blue and green capsules. I took one with the water, and when she went to return the glass, I swallowed another one dry. She never knew. I managed to cope at the service, but collapsed in a puddle of tears when I got home.

So, what was new now? Well, for one thing, closing in on seventy, I'd seen a lot more death. It didn't make it any easier, just a little more understandable. But I was having a tough time with Charlie. Except for the booze, Charlie took good care of himself. His years as a lineman, doing hard work in all kinds of weather, gave him the look of someone like a… lumberjack. That was the image I had. When he smoked, he looked like the Marlboro Man. To see him begin to slide now, and knowing from my experience with Barbara what he could become, was devastating.

I made coffee, put stale bread in the toaster, and sat at the table with my head in my hands. Then pushed aside my feelings with the coffee and toast, swept crumbs into my hand to flush down the sink, and headed back upstairs, thinking a shower would bring me back to life. It didn't. It was still early, so I took the long way to Charlie's condo and drove past the bowling alley. That was a wrong move. It put too many memories on active alert. *Shit! Why Charlie?* I had no answer to that.

On the other hand, he came whistling down the sidewalk to my car, pulled open the door, and said, "Wazz up?" He was full of piss and vinegar like we were going to the golf course, not someplace where they would fill him up with toxic chemicals and cause him to puke his guts out.

"Aren't you bright-eyed and bushy-tailed," I said, making a stupid statement that I had suddenly recalled from my father. It was going to be one of those days. "Sleep well?"

"Why the fuck not," he answered with a big, shit-eating grin. I wondered if he had been drinking, but decided it was just Charlie.

Not much more was said until we reached the hospital. "You know the drill," I said.

"You bet." He left the car and started whistling as he strode to the automatic door without looking back.

***

I wished I'd brought a book to read, but this morning I wasn't in the mood and I figured, with the shitty night I'd had, I would just put my head back and dream on. That didn't work, so I dug out the Ford Owner's Manual and began to learn something about the car. That was worth doing, but an hour later, I had learned all I cared to know. Not wanting to lose my parking space, I decided to walk to the main entrance and buy a newspaper. I had never been to this hospital; we used the older Southside West building. A large lobby was naturally lit in the daytime, with the sun streaming through a glass dome and streaking the terrazzo floor with colored lines.

There was a coffee bar with an adjacent gift shop on the far side of the lobby. I got a coffee, a cinnamon raisin bagel, and *The New York Times*. The lobby was so much more comfortable than the car that I decided to stay here and fell asleep in the chair, only waking when my cell phone sounded.

Thinking it was Charlie, I didn't look at the display, just blurted, "I'll be right there; I fell asleep in the lobby."

"What?" It was a call from Marilyn.

I tried to laugh it off. "Hey, just kidding, how are you?"

"Where are you?" she said in a voice that demanded a straight answer.

"Downtown," I answered, even though there were hospital intercom sounds in the background, and a siren-wailing ambulance had just driven past the door.

"No, you're not. It sounds like a hospital. Are you alright?"

"Yeah, I'm alright; I'm here with Charlie."

"Is Charlie alright?" Marilyn liked Charlie best of all my friends; they always seemed to laugh together.

"He's okay. Just a little stomach thing... you know... booze-itis, I think it's called."

"I understand, of course, he could have a problem with all his drinking... nothing serious, I hope." I could have answered that question. But when she added, "Not cancer?" I hesitated, and she read my delay like an open book.

"Dex, does he have cancer?"

I was stuck. "Maybe, a little."

"Dex, there is no fucking *little* with stomach cancer!" She didn't swear very often.

"He's having chemo today. A tumor on his liver."

She was silent for a minute, and I knew she had started crying. "Oh, Jesus... Dex, why didn't you call me? I'm so sorry for him... and for you, Dex."

"Thanks, Mar, thank you for saying that. The doctors are right on this, so there could be a good outcome." I wondered if that lie had sounded real. I didn't want to ask, but said, "What about your mom, anything good there?"

"Same, same... Dex, I feel terrible about this... I have to go... I'll call you."

She ended the call without hearing me say, "I miss you."

***

It was another hour before Charlie was released. I jogged back to the garage after his call, and when I returned, he was sitting in a wheelchair at the curb, being tended to by a young woman in pink scrubs. The back of his left hand was covered with a taped-on gauze pad. He offered a tip to the girl, but she thanked him and refused, saying it was not allowed.

After he settled, I said, "Tell me."

"Not bad, they wanted to put a port in me for future chemo. The nurse freaked when I told her there was no next chemo and she called for a doctor. Nice guy from India. I think he understood. But they did a great job on my feet."

"Your feet?"

"Yeah, this woman does foot massages while you're lying there; thirty-five bucks, not bad. And they have a big TV."

"What can I do for you now?"

"I think I'd better go home, Dex. I'm starting to feel a little woozy."

I left him at his condo and watched him go up the sidewalk, hunched a little, not whistling anymore.

When I got home, I went to my chair and sat there, swiveling slowly left and right, trying to make sense of this senseless day.

I guessed my dad was lucky; he'd had the same shitty heart his father had, and when he reached his due date, he collapsed and died at the store. I was at the bank with the day's deposit when he dropped. Dad had been waiting on Bob Ricker; selling him some new pruning shears. Bob was a retired fireman who knew precisely what to do in that emergency, but it was not enough.

When we were both a little shitfaced after a softball game, Bob told me that Dad was dead before he hit the floor. "It was a good way to go, Dex. He dropped like a rock."

My mother was a different story. She phased out over the years, beginning with forgetting, no big deal. But it started to look serious when she forgot to put her shoes on to go out in the snow. When she was finally hospitalized in an Alzheimer's wing, she had no idea who I was.

I hoped it would end soon for Marilyn's mom. I meant it; I wasn't trying to be selfish and draw Marilyn back.

I decided to get some Chinese take-out, and checked off several items from the Bamboo Palace menu I kept on my phone. When the kid delivered, I tipped him twenty bucks, trying to soothe my sadness with money.

Chapter 10

On the way back from the hospital, Charlie asked me to call the guys, saying, "I don't think I can handle it, Dex, you know, fucking up their day and the sympathy and all that shit."

"No problem, I'll give it to them straight, no sugar coating."

"Best way."

***

I called Tom first, and got the reaction I expected: silence, profanity, grief, then, "What can we do for him, Dex… what can we do?"

"The best we can do is honor his feelings, Tom; he's ready to die. That's exactly what he told me. It's not that he doesn't give a shit; it's like a form of acceptance. He said he's had a full life, and it's time to try something different. So how's that for being Charlie, *try something different*? He also wanted you to call your lawyer, Marty Kaspersky, to set up a meeting with him and his accountant, Ben Doyle. He didn't say A-S-A-P, but I think that needs to be done."

"I'll call Marty immediately. I just talked with him, so I know he's in his office."

"Thanks, Tom, keep in touch. I've gotta call Dickie now."

I called Richard Lane, MD. "Dr. Lane is with a patient right now, Mr. Phillips, but he should be available in about fifteen minutes. Should I have him call you then?"

"Please, and tell him it's important."

Dickie had retired several years ago. But he came to his former office, now occupied by his doctor daughter, to provide pro bono work on indigent patients weekly.

***

When Dickie called, his reaction was much like Tom's, except he added, "Sonofabitch. And I'm supposed to be a fucking doctor. I never saw it. I never fucking saw it."

I knew he was upset because he didn't often swear.

"What can we do, Dex? Who's his doctor? Maybe I can talk with him?"

"I don't think he'd want that, Dick; he's determined to do it his way. Maybe he feels penance for all the drunkenness, the broken marriages, whatever. But, Jesus, I hope not. I'll keep you posted, and Tom's having his lawyer meet with Charlie's accountant at his request. Charlie's still pretty much on top of things. I'll call you when I hear something new."

I sat back, finished the rest of my General Tso dinner, washed it down with the remainder of a Heineken, and felt I needed to work on the book.

***

I sat in my office chair and thought about sports, kid sports. I found a picture of me standing with a hockey stick, gloves, and shin pads, looking like I was about to make a slap shot in the living room. The dog's backend could be seen to my left and my father's foot to the right. I assumed my mother took the picture. I loved hockey as a kid and was probably about ten years old in this picture. We skated on a small pond about a block from my house. It was called Warner's Pond, but no one seemed to know why. I called this narrative:

THE POND

We couldn't wait for the ice to freeze hard enough to skate on. So, we'd start testing its strength each winter by throwing big rocks on the ice. When they remained on top, we would venture out slowly with long sticks to pound on the ice until it cracked. There was always someone brave enough to cautiously walk out with a rope around their waist and at least two of us holding the other end near the shore. Unfortunately, someone always went through the ice and had to be pulled out.

Warner's Pond was shallow, perhaps no more than four feet at its deepest part, and because it was sheltered from the sun, it tended to freeze early in the season. A small brook filled the pond from its southern edge by the big rock. This area was last to freeze and often was thin enough to break through. That is why we used the dog.

It got dark too soon after school because of the surrounding trees. Still, on Saturday morning, we got there early, set up goal markers, usually just rocks, and played hockey until we couldn't stand up.

The longest distance ran north to south with the pond layout, so the goals were at those ends. When a puck got past the south goal, it was usually over thin ice. Then we used the dog, who was only too happy to fetch it. Even when he broke through, he never lost the puck. His front legs would break ice until he could stand and return on top, shaking the water until icicles formed on his belly and tail. He loved it; Bucky, the wonder dog. The only problem was when he decided: why fetch and retrieve, why not grab and go? So, a large part of the game was to keep the puck away from him in the first place.

My biggest hockey problem began when I was fourteen and grew six inches in a year. The following year, another six put me head and shoulders above my friends, pushing me into basketball. We already had the backboard and hoop on the garage, and when Dad had the guy come to paint the keyhole, I knew my focus would be b-ball. I spent hours practicing alone or playing "horse." I dribbled down the sidewalks to school, right hand going, left hand coming home. I played good high school ball on a good team in the best conference in the state. I just wasn't good enough for college.

These memories brought me into a better mood. I'd been ping-ponging between Charlie and Marilyn, and the childhood thoughts freed me to move on.

I needed to focus on the book, not keep dicking around. So, right after dinner, I decided, I would sit and write with determination.

That's what I told myself. But this is what I actually did: I decided on a Mexican dinner with enough ingredients to make four tacos. I use two tortilla shells, one inside the other, and went heavy on the salsa and sour cream. They sure were messy, but super tasty, especially with the Dos Equis I was drinking from the bottle.

Still with intentions to write, I thought it best to let the tacos settle, so I turned on PBS. It was a documentary on World War I ambulance drivers. I looked for my grandad, but was unsure if I could pick him out. I did see footage of Ernest Hemingway and was a little ashamed that I was not in my office working. But I had gained some knowledge, had two more beers, and decided to call it a night, promising myself a hard day's work on the book *mañana.*

***

I woke Thursday morning knowing I'd had a weird dream; something about Charlie. It took me a while to recall what it was.

Finally, I remembered. Our team was bowling for the championship, and each strike we made would reduce Charlie's tumor. Tom, Dick, and I kept rolling strikes, high-fiving after each score. Charlie could only throw gutter balls. Three of us were going to give him a cure. If only it could be that easy.

That didn't get me off to a great start, but as I had promised myself, I went to my chair to write. The problem was, I just sat there, staring out the window, watching a squirrel try to raid the bird feeder. I had mounted this on a metal pole, but the little bastards could still climb it. So, I coated the top two feet with Vaseline. I figured it wouldn't be toxic, but it did stop the seed raids. As often as I watched for a squirrel to attempt the climb, I only saw it once. It was pretty funny, but I felt sorry for the squirrel and threw some seed on the ground. Why not?

I'd made some notes during the PBS documentary. I searched for additional information by going to Google and researching the American Field Service. Somewhere among those daring and courageous men and women was my grandad. I became more convinced that he had known guys like Hemingway and Dos Passos because they had all served on the Italian front. The sense of adventure that led these young Americans to volunteer for this dangerous duty was profound and not without casualties. Two hundred ninety-six Red Cross nurses and one hundred seventy ambulance drivers were killed. The more I got into this, the more fascinating the topic was, and I was beginning to see the roots of my book. I knew my dad had some papers and letters from his father, which were probably upstairs in the attic. As I got up to look for them, my phone sounded, and the display said *CHUCK.*

"Hey man, wazz up?" My usual joking greeting for him.

"Doin' good, man, doin' good." He was trying hard to sound good. I didn't believe him. "I met with that lawyer, Kaspersky, Tom's guy, and my accountant, Benny, last night."

"Sounds like you've got a handle on things."

"I have, brother, I have." I wondered if he was drinking or just taking the pain meds.

"I decided to ask. "What are they doing for you med-wise?" I thought a made-up word was appropriate, since Charlie would probably give me a made-up answer.

"Nothin' special, just some pain stuff."

"Are you drinking?"

"Why not?"

I tried to be stern about this without thinking it through. "Jesus. Chuck, that's dangerous. You combine booze with those heavy-duty cancer pain pills; it could kill you."

His wild laughter pierced my soul. I could not believe my stupidity. The laughter continued until it turned into tears, then hiccups, and he killed the phone.

I stared at my phone and thought about punching myself in the mouth with it when it lit up again: *CHUCK.* Before he could speak, I was into an apology. I called myself everything from asshole to zasshole. By the time I finished on myself, he was in hysterics, but this was a good laugh, and I joined in with him.

He told me he had hired a private nurse when he settled down.

"Hey, that's an excellent idea." I tried to sound upbeat, but I knew what that meant: not much time.

"Yeah, I got her starting Monday. She'll live in the guest room twenty-four seven. She sounded okay on the phone, maybe a little old, like fifties or something. I hope she's got big tits.

"You are fucking incorrigible. So, she can monitor your meds and stuff?"

"Oh yeah, she's in direct contact with the doc. She does bloodwork and stuff like that. So, it sounds like a good deal."

"It does; that sounds like a good deal." But then, I realized I was repeating his comment, and the conversation would not last much longer.

"Hey, anyway, I just wanted to touch base."

"Why don't I come over?" I offered.

"Not trying to be rude, Dex, but I don't think I can handle visits. If you know what I mean."

"I know what you mean. Take care, Chuck, take care." I killed the call and hit myself in the head with the phone… *take care.*

Chapter 11

I took a clean sheet of copy paper into the kitchen, got a coffee can, traced a circle with a Magic Marker, then wrote *TAKE CARE* in the ring and drew a diagonal line through it. I took this back into my office and taped it to the desk lamp. Satisfied with my anti-slogan handiwork, I went back to the kitchen. I poured some Jim Beam into a water glass, raised it high, and saluted in the direction of Chuck's condo. "Peace to you, my friend." I sat the bourbon back on the table, idly pushing a spoon around.

I was just getting my shit together when my cell lit up — a two-word text from *MARILYN.*

Mom died.

I didn't know how long I sat there, but it was starting to get dark. The glass was empty, my emotions were drained, and I thought I would puke. I got some wheat bread out of the breadbox and ate two slices, then cupped my hands under the cold water and splashed my face, making a mess around the sink. I switched the ceiling light on, filled the former bourbon glass with water, and sat down again.

It was clear Marilyn felt she couldn't control her emotions for a voice call. She hated to text. After years in an office environment with short, rounded, buffed fingernails, she went nail-crazy when she retired. It was as if she were throwing off the shackles of her former life.

She was a regular at Fingers & Feet, a nail salon on Brady Street. Her nails were always long and pointed, varnished in various colors, and coated with sparkly stuff or appliques. She loved it and avoided damage by refusing to text. I didn't text because I was finger clumsy, but I needed to try.

So, so sorry. Words cannit expres it. Mt thoughts r With u and ur sisters. Please, please, call me when U can. We need 2 talk.

I didn't tell her I now had an email account. There was plenty of time for that.

I grabbed a jar of peanut butter, a spoon, and a beer, and went to the living room to distract myself with a ball game on TV. That didn't work, so I tried a movie, watching *Mary Poppins* for the umpteenth time. That helped; I placed myself *high above the chimney tops,* where I imagined Charlie was cured and Marilyn's mother was not dead.

***

On Friday morning, I didn't feel too bad, considering too much to drink, too much sadness, too little sleep, and insufficient food. However, I had to eat something substantial and made a big cheese omelet with diced red and green peppers and link sausage and wheat toast. I hoped I could keep it down.

An hour later, feeling better, I showered, shaved, and dressed to get a sympathy card to send to Arizona. The sheer volume of cards in the Hallmark store was an ample testament to how shitty the world could be for some people. I felt sorry for all of them. I chose what I thought was an appropriate card and drove to the Post Office for stamps and mailing.

I was third in the stamp-buying line when a cheerful voice behind me said, "Hi, Mr. Phillips." I turned to see Emma beaming up at me.

"Hey, what a surprise again. You seem to be everywhere I go."

"I was next door at the cleaners when I saw you drive in. How are you?"

"I'm okay; kind of busy right now."

Before Emma could respond, the postal clerk said, "Sir, you're next."

She explained the Forever Stamps, and I bought a book that seemed like a good deal. She informed me that, with the weekend, the card would not get to Arizona until Tuesday. So, I decided to send it by Express Mail and went to the table to fill out the necessary info on the envelope. I didn't know when Emma left or where she went, but I was relieved by her absence.

I stopped and got a loaf of French bread on the way home.

***

Her car was parked at the curb in front of my house. My first thought was to drive by and wait her out. Then, I thought she might wander around the backyard, so I drove in and saw the back door was open. "Oh, shit!"

I was in such a hurry to get out of the car that I took a few quick steps before I realized I hadn't shut off the engine. "Shit!"

She wasn't in the kitchen. "Emma," I called. No sound. I quickly went to the office door, but she wasn't there. "Oh, Jesus! Emma, where are you?" I yelled the question, but like a good lawyer, I knew the answer and took the stairs two at a time.

She was on my bed, fully clothed, except for her sneakers, which were aligned on the floor. She was wearing tight jeans and a sweatshirt bearing a Minnie Mouse logo. On her back, feet together, arms stretched to her sides and her head centered between the two pillows, looking like a living crucifix.

"What the hell are you doing here?"

She smiled and pursed her lips in a kiss before saying, "Waiting for you."

I thought my head would explode. "Jesus H. Christ, I don't believe this!" I backed up a few steps shaking my head. "Emma, let's get real, I'm sixty-nine years old, and you're a goddamn child."

She raised her head and spit out, "Child! Do you think I'm a child? Take a look at these." She started to pull up the sweatshirt, and I ran from the room. I went to the kitchen as if it were a sanctuary, closed the back door, and pressed my head against it, hoping to gain some wisdom from the wooden frame. I thought about calling the cops, but knew she could lie and destroy me. I thought about leaving the house, but was afraid of the damage she might do to it… or herself. *Shit!* I was trying to figure out other options when the front door opened… and closed. She was gone.

I ran to the front entry and locked the door, looking out just in time to see her VW bug drive off.

Walking back to my office, I pulled out my cell and called *TOM B.* Then, I sat in my chair and swiveled around to face the door, afraid she might suddenly reappear.

Tom finally answered, "Dex."

"Hey Tom, I've got a big problem."

"I'm listening."

I told him the whole sordid story without interruption. Then, when I finished, he said, "Why not get out of there for a while and take a vacation? Maybe she'll give up if she comes around and the place is empty."

"That sounds good, but we've got league starting this week."

"That's no problem; my cousin Russell is on board to… to take Charlie's place. And we're allowed a sub for an emergency. So don't worry about it, I'll find someone. Why not visit Marilyn?"

"Her mother just died. She texted me this morning."

"Oh, shit… hey, you guys have been together for what… three years? She could use your support. Call her, fly down… it's warm there. I'll swing by your house while you're gone; keep an eye on things."

"Tom, you always were the man with the plan. I'll call her, but I'm going anyway. I need to get away from here. I don't mean to intrude. Thanks, good buddy. Great idea. I'll keep you posted."

***

I hadn't been on a plane in years. I knew tickets could be bought online, but didn't feel comfortable with that. So, I went to Destinations Travel in the Crossroad Mall and booked a flight with their help.

When I got home, I put my phone on the desk, sat down, and stared at it for a while, trying to figure out how this call would go. Finally, I dialed. I realized my jaw was tight as the call went to Marilyn's voicemail. *This is Marilyn B. I'll call you back when able.*

I shrunk from her terse message. Marilyn was a caring person, but things like this sometimes made her seem severe. In reality, she was a little shy, and this was one of her defenses.

I tried to be as cheerful as possible and not let my voice show the anxiety I felt down to my feet. "Hey, Mar, how are things in the sunny Southwest? I just wanted to let you know I decided to try it. Arizona, that is. I'm flying down there tomorrow. I just need a little vacation, so I'm doing that. I'm flying into Phoenix, and I'll get a room when I get there and call you. Again, sorry about your mom. My best to you and your sisters. See ya."

Five minutes later, she called back, and I let it go to voicemail, wincing slightly as her voice came through the speaker.

Dex, sometimes you really piss me off. You're going to fly down here and get a room. What the hell are you thinking? I will pick you up, and you will come back here to the ranch; that's final. Call me with your flight details. Sometimes, I just want to kick you, but I'm looking forward to seeing you right now. It's been a while. Call me.

Sometimes, I thought I needed a kick.

I reveled in her words, *looking forward to seeing you. It's been a while.* It had been a while since I'd had something to feel good about. "Yes!" I punched the air, whooped with happiness, did a couple of 360s in the chair, and called her back.

The best defense is a good offense, so before she could speak, I said, "Do you still want to kick me?"

"You are something else. Did you really think you could fly down here, get a hotel room, and what… call me once in a while?"

"I didn't want to intrude, you know, funeral and all that."

"Dex, she's been dying for a year. It's over. We've had our cry. She's in a better place, Dex. Now we get on with living. There will be a service on Thursday, and I want you to come. We want you to come. Linda and Emily want to meet… my man. Give me your flight details. We'll pick you up."

I read the travel agent's summary details and started to say goodbye. She stopped me.

"How's Charlie?"

I knew better than to lie, so I stupidly said, "He's bowling in the last frame. We'll talk about it when I see you."

I cut the call short, giving her no chance to say, "Take care."

Chapter 12

I hadn't been on an airplane in years, and I was a little overwhelmed by the crowds, the security, the check-in procedures, and the seat, which seemed to have a lot less legroom than I recalled. I was sitting between a nurse flying home to Utah and a sporting goods salesman on a business trip. Both people were cordial, but we didn't talk much. The nurse slept, the salesman worked on his laptop, and I read a Martha Grimes novel, trying to get comfortable with my long legs.

We had a short layover in Chicago, where the nurse deplaned. That seat remained empty on the flight to Phoenix, making things a little more comfortable. There were no weather issues on the trip, and as we approached Phoenix Sky Harbor International, I was startled by the brilliance of the desert landscape. The blue sky and megawatt sun were like nothing I had ever imagined. It made Connecticut seem as if it were painted on gray cardboard — and that was on a good day. I had never thought of bringing sunglasses.

The terminal buildings looked like something out of a Hollywood blockbuster film. As I exited the terminal, I saw Marilyn standing with a group of uniformed professional drivers, holding a sign that read: *DEXTER*. Marilyn didn't joke much, so this made me laugh so hard that people around me shied away from this crazy person.

I liked what I saw. She was Southwest-dressed, in a skirt of varied colors that appeared to be of Native American patterns. She wore a sleeveless cotton top that showed her still-good figure and trim, suntanned arms. I smiled so hard it hurt, and I waved like an idiot. Then we met. We hugged and kissed twice before she released me, holding me with outstretched arms and a beautiful smile. One of the drivers behind her gave me a thumbs-up, and I nodded and kissed her again. This was going to be a beautiful day.

As we came to the baggage area, I saw my bag making the bend and sprinted to the conveyor to grab it before it disappeared through the flaps again. As I walked back to Marilyn, I noticed one of the TSA guys was closely observing me.

We walked out of the terminal with my arm around her waist. Nothing had been said; we felt comfortable, and words were unnecessary. She was leaning into me with a softness that said it all. She had called her sister, Linda, to make her way over from short-term parking while I was getting my bag. Linda was waiting at the curb in a white GMC Denali. I opened the front door for Marilyn, then got in the back with my bag.

"Dex, so good to finally meet you." Linda turned and stuck a hand with a gold charm bracelet between the seats. I was surprised by her firm grip and how much she resembled her older sister. The same hazel eyes and freckles across the nose were visible, even through her golfer's tan. The same long, brown hair in a pony-tail, currently pulled through the back loop of a golf cap. I could see she had a similar stature and compact, athletic body as her sister. She was a few years younger than Marilyn and looked like she had just played eighteen holes at the club. The car behind us honked, and we drove off to start "Dexter's Wonderful Southwest Adventure."

I reached over the seat just to touch Marilyn again, and she grabbed my hand, squeezed it, and kissed it. A shiver went through me.

On the way north along *AZ 87*, Linda kept up a running monologue as we passed this or that of natural or historical significance. Marilyn didn't say much, but I could feel her happiness. When I thought about us over the weeks before she left, I realized the strain she had been under with her mother's waning health.

We passed the city of Fountain Hills, and just to the west of that, beside the edge of the Tonto National Park, was the ranch. I didn't know if they use the word palatial down here, but as we turned into the drive to their home, I said to myself, *at least "Rancho Grande."* This place looked like the month's featured property in a Southwest edition of *Architectural Digest.* I felt embarrassed about my Connecticut home.

The driveway ended with a cul de sac in front of a covered porch on a large, stucco, single-level building.

As we got out of the car, Emily came trotting down the stone path, right up to me, hand out, and said, "Dex!"

She kissed my cheek while holding my hand, and said with a grin and great enthusiasm, "Hi, I'm Emily, the youngest sister." I figured she was a couple of years younger than Linda, maybe late fifties, but like her sisters, she had the same hair, complexion, eyes, and build. She was dressed in a pink and white golf outfit.

Both sisters had been divorced for years. Marilyn said, with mock anger, "Get your hands off him. He's mine," then wrapped an arm around my waist. We all laughed and headed into the house after I got my bag.

Inside was like nothing I had ever imagined. It was truly magnificent. It had an open floor plan, deep wooden beams, and stunning desert décor, with many antiques from nineteenth-century ranch life. The sisters left us to make drinks, and Marilyn, still with an arm around my waist, said, "Daddy was a home builder in this area, and this was his pride and joy." I saw a framed photo and a plaque with a gold-toned metal plate mounted on the wall, among many other plaques and two shelves of golf trophies.

JAMES E. FITZGERALD

PHOENIX AREA BUILDER OF THE YEAR

"That's your dad," I said, not as a question, because it was easy to see the resemblance.

"That's Daddy; he was a wonderful man in every way you can imagine. He built this house with love and loved the people he built it for. He didn't deserve cancer, Dex. He didn't deserve to die young." I saw the tears starting in the corners of her eyes, and she turned her head away, still holding onto me. Then said, "Let's get you settled."

We went down a wide corridor to the rear of the bedroom wing, feeling the cool breeze coming in off the back patio and pool. And walking toward us was the cat. She came right to me. I picked her up, hugged her, and smoothed her fur while she mewed softly in my ear. She rubbed her head into my ankle when I put her down and then took off on a cat mission. She must like it here, I thought.

I expected to be set up in a guest room, and when we entered what was, apparently, Marilyn's bedroom, I stopped and looked at her. She could read the question on my face.

"We're all adults here, Dex." She laughed and kissed me, saying, "Make yourself comfortable. The bathroom's through there. And when you've changed into something more Arizona, come out to the pool. The girls are making margaritas." She blew me an air kiss as she backed out of the room, the cat following.

***

I changed into a Red Sox tee and the dorky surfer shorts and Tevas I was now glad I had packed, trying to figure out what to wear in the sun. I pulled my Mountainview Driving Range ballcap low, trying to soften the glare. I needed to get some sunglasses fast.

Marilyn had gone elsewhere and changed into a two-piece bathing suit, which could be argued was cut for a younger woman. Still, she was in such good shape that it was appropriate and stunning. She was lying on a double-wide chaise lounge, and when I pulled up a single chair, she patted the cushion next to her, saying, "Get over here." This must be a dream.

Linda came out carrying a pitcher of margaritas with lots of ice and lime slices floating on the top. The stemmed glasses had wide, salt-encrusted rims. "Em's making snacks," she said, putting down the tray and pouring into the glasses. There was a sizeable umbrella, which she adjusted to cover my pinkish-white body in the shade. Marilyn had developed a lovely copper tan in the short time she had been here.

Emily came out pushing a stainless-steel cart with plates of hors d'oeuvres, including a metal basket of spicy chicken wings set over a low Sterno flame. So, *this* was how the other half lived.

Linda pointed a remote toward a console mounted on the patio wall, and music began. She lowered the volume and looked at my surprise, saying, "What, Dex, they don't have pools and patios in Connecticut?"

"This late in October, we don't even have green grass. I'm overwhelmed by all of this."

The girls laughed, and Marilyn said, "You ain't seen nuthin' yet." I looked at her, and the wink and smile told me to expect the best.

***

The pitcher was empty, the Sterno flame extinguished, and the sisters had gone to the club for barbecue night. I moved off the chaise into a chair and faced Marilyn, saying, "I need to tell you about Charlie."

She handled it well. There were some tears, but she understood it was what Charlie wanted for himself, perhaps better than I did. Then, feeling like it was time, I asked about her mother.

She took a deep breath, blew it out slowly, sat more upright, and said, "It's over; it was a long, drawn-out agony for her and us. But, frankly, Dex, we're all glad it's over. Maybe that sounds callous, but you've been there, I think, with Barbara." She paused, waiting for my response.

All I could say was, "I understand. Let's move on. I saw your dad's picture and plaque in the great room. He was a Fitzgerald, and you…"

"I'm a Fitzgerald, too."

I made a stupid kind of questioning gesture with my hands.

"Brewer was my husband's name."

I sat there, open-mouthed… started to say something… but she continued.

"And we had a daughter… she would have been nineteen next week."

I started to get up, not knowing what else to do.

"Sit down, Dex. You might as well hear the whole story."

I sat, leaning toward her with a concentration that felt like I had turned to stone.

"Jack and I could not have children, so we adopted Amelia from the San Carlos Apache reservation north of here. She was two years old when she came to us. She grew up pretty, strong, and smart, and planned to attend Med School. She and Jack were driving home from her dance lessons five years ago when he got a cell call. He pulled onto the breakdown lane to take the call…" She paused to wipe away some tears. "A truck… eighteen-wheeler… driver fell asleep... it went right over the top of them. It crushed them, Dex… crushed them into nothing." The tears flowed, and she covered her face with a towel off the back of the chaise.

What the hell could I do? I wanted to hold her, say something, do something to ease her pain. But, instead, I walked away, knowing at that point, I couldn't do anything. I had been there before.

I wandered around the pool, looking at the mosaic design shimmering on the bottom, trying to make sense of all this grief. When I returned, she had recovered her emotions and looked up at me with red-rimmed eyes, a runny nose, and a sly smile. Then said, "Let's take a shower."

Chapter 13

I had entered a new universe, a world of sun and warmth, beauty, and wealth. And I had a new woman. Marilyn was a child of the Southwest who was lost in Connecticut. She had come there with her grief two years before I met her. A pain and experience she had never revealed in the years we'd been together. I always suspected Marilyn had more history than she cared to share, but that was hers to hold. Not mine to open and judge. But here in her home, she seemed to have shed the wraps of her tragedy and become an outgoing — even passionate — woman I hadn't known existed. But I welcomed it with all my being.

Of course, this magnificent house had luxurious facilities. The en suite bathroom had a glass-enclosed shower that could accommodate a choral group. There were multiple shower heads on the ceiling and lined up vertically in the tiled wall. A touchpad controlled the water temperature and flow. Music came from somewhere. She had a variety of body washes and shampoos shelved on niches in the stone slab wall at the head of the enclosure; we used several. It was like showering in a rainforest, like something I could only dream of. Finally, we dried off with towels from a heated rack.

Also in the bathroom was a large Jacuzzi tub set in an alcove with small, recessed colored lights tucked into a lowered ceiling that made me think of a tropical cave. When I moved to go there, she caught my wrist and said, "Later." So, I followed her to the bed like a puppy on a leash.

***

I needed to get some clothes. I'd never expected to be in an environment like this and had come here unprepared. We drove twenty miles to the Southland Mall in a Chrysler convertible that was parked in the four-bay garage next to Marilyn's Connecticut sedan. My taste in clothing was practical and cheap. Marilyn picked out what I needed. I left Salomon's Casual Male wearing pleat-front chinos, a loose-fitting linen shirt, and some basketweave sandals with rope soles. She told me to wait out front with the packages while she went into a jewelry store. She returned, placed a wide turquoise-and-silver bracelet on my left wrist, and said, "Welcome to the new world." And kissed me hard in front of a lot of onlooking shoppers.

We had dinner at Whiskey Pete's, and it felt like I was back on the range in 1890. We had steaks and curly fries, grilled corn, and flatbread with several kinds of salsa. This was the best dinner of my life, not just because of the food, but because Marilyn sat close and put a hand on my thigh. Who was this woman?

***

Her sisters were home when we got back, along with a guy named Brian, a project manager for the construction company founded by their father. Linda was now the CEO. Building plans were rolled up and leaning against Brian's chair. We all had a beer, and he gave me a verbal tour of the area and the business of Fitzgerald Builders. Brian offered to take me with him in the morning, but knowing I would be exhausted, I declined and said I'd love to do it another day. I meant it.

***

Yes, I was exhausted in the morning. When I awoke, Marilyn was gone. Her swimsuit was missing from the bathroom. I had intended to get more appropriate swimwear for myself and some sunglasses last night at the mall, but I was so overwhelmed with everything else, I forgot. I decided I would do that later.

I put on the dorky surfer shorts and crept toward the pool, hiding behind a potted cactus. As she swam to the far end with slow, smooth strokes, I waited for her turn and let her get most of the way back. Then ran, screaming like an idiot and cannonballed her. When she stopped laughing, she splashed me and yelled, "Idiot!"

***

The next few days stretched my imagination into a new dimension. The lazy mornings poolside and short afternoon trips to see natural wonders, museums, and commercial tourist attractions were overwhelming. I finally got my sunglasses, not the cheap plastic ones I had picked up, but the Ray-Ban aviators with amber lenses that Marilyn put on me. We ate on the patio each night, where I showed my culinary skills to her sisters. The sunsets were beyond anything I had ever seen, and there was no rain.

I had been here a week and was thinking of staying forever. I had the pool net out, picking some insect debris off the water when my phone sounded in my shirt pocket: *TOM B.*

I accepted the call willingly, ready to tough out whatever the message.

"Hey, Tom."

"Hey, Dex, hate to bother you with this call, but it needs to be done."

"Go ahead."

"Well, Charlie only had to spend eighteen-hundred bucks for the nurse, so I'm sure he was happy about that."

"You saying Chuck died?"

"Yeah, Dex, that's what I'm saying. I just couldn't find the words. Nurse Diane called me about an hour ago. She said he passed in the night with no trauma. He just kept sleeping." I thought about Bucky. "Here's the rest of that. He had Marty draw up a will and wanted it read while he was still alive… you'll get a kick out of this."

"I'm listening."

"Well, he left the bulk of his estate to his boys, which was good. That old bastard started buying electric company stock with his first paycheck when he was nineteen and never stopped. His estate was worth over two million, which is not bad for a guy with only a high school education." He continued on, "He left his former wives each a grand, suggesting they take their husbands to Foxwoods for a party night." I started laughing at that. "But here's the real kicker, he left you, me, and Dickie each one dollar with the stipulation we *use it wisely.*" I was laughing so hard I had to use the pool net for support. Marilyn had come out on the patio.

Tom hesitated, then added, "Now, on to the next thing… Emma."

I sucked in my breath and moved further away from Marilyn. "Go on."

"Well, to begin with, that's not her name. She took that from some book by Jane Ashton."

"Austen."

"Excuse me."

"The author was Jane Austen."

"Whatever, her real name is Darlene Spector."

"How the hell do you know this?" I was moving closer to the deep end of the pool.

"I drove by your place Monday afternoon and spotted a VW parked behind the house. I could see the ass end of it, so I snuck around back, and she was sleeping on your chaise lounge —"

I interrupted, "What the hell did you do?" I was bent over the phone, whispering.

"Shut up, and I'll tell you. I called Marty, and he called someone he knew at the station. They sent a cruiser and a female officer. She woke up Ms. Spector and took her downtown."

"Holy shit!"

"There's more… how old did she say she was?"

"Twenty-one."

"She's eighteen." Tom could feel my anxiety. "There's more… Broken home, the father left when she was twelve, mother's a druggie living on public assistance. for years. Then, two years ago, the kid got into a child services group home, where she tested pretty damn smart and got a GED at sixteen. There was a good chance she could have gone to college on some sort of scholarship, but here's the shit about all this. She turned eighteen last February, and the day after, it's *sayonara* from Child Services. You're out on your ass and out in the street. This is a crappy system we've got."

"So, what happened?" I had now moved to the opposite side of the pool, dragging the net without noticing.

"The usual, she was stopped for shoplifting at Target, but somehow talked her way out of it and got a warning. Then she tried her luck on the street, and the first guy she tagged was a vice cop. He brought her in and scared the shit out of her. Then, being a good cop with two daughters of his own, he got her a room at St. Martin's Church. There are still four old nuns living there to keep an eye on her, and she'll go back there if you don't file trespassing charges."

"Jesus, what do you think?"

"That's what I told them. She's on her way back to St. Martin's as we speak."

"Oh shit, do you think the nuns can handle her?"

"Obviously, you didn't go to Catholic school."

"Okay, but what's the long game for her? This is only a band-aid."

"There's no solution to this unless she can get somewhere for counseling, education, social skills, whatever. But now you're talking private, someplace like Meadowbrook Academy. Now you're talking real money, Dex."

"I don't care. Can you do this for me...for her?"

"I'll get Marty working on it."

"I'll transfer some money this morning and send you a check for ten thousand. Will that get it rolling?"

"I'll get it done and get back to you when I know more. Again, give my regards to Marilyn. Take care, Dex."

"You're the best, Tom." I was too overwhelmed to be pissed off at the, *take care.*

I needed a drink. I called across the pool to Marilyn as I went toward the kitchen, "You want a cold one?" She shook her head *no* and went back to reading something, the cat lying on her lap.

I had just gotten a beer from the fridge when my phone sounded again, an unlisted number on the screen. *What the hell?* I answered, "Dex Phillips."

"Mr. Phillips, this is Diane… I was Mr. Osbourne's nurse… I'm sorry to tell you he passed this early morning. He was with the Lord when I checked on him at six. He apparently died peacefully; his covers were all in place, and there was no sign that he'd been uncomfortable."

"Thank you for calling, Diane."

There's another thing, Mr. Phillips… he wrote out a statement for me to read to you. As a Christian, I don't use these words. This is a quote, Mr. Phillips, *Dex, you were the best… motherfucking friend, a guy, could ever have.* That's all, Mr. Phillips. Those are his words, not mine."

"Thank you, Diane."

When Marilyn got to the kitchen to see what was going on, I was laughing so hard I could barely stand. I managed to pull the tab off the can, and the shaken beer was foaming all over the place. I rained tears and snot and could hardly breathe. Marilyn just stood there at first, confused. Then, she giggled at me, and the two of us collapsed in each other's arms. I picked her up, went out, and threw both of us into the pool. The cat watched from her perch on top of the chaise.

Chapter 14

The funeral service was serene but straightforward and emotionally moving, with family and about twelve others in attendance. The chapel was flower-filled and cool, with soft background music floating throughout. There was no priest or pastor.

Marilyn gave the first eulogy as the oldest daughter, speaking eloquently about her mother's loving and charitable life. She had worked on the San Carlos Reservation and with patients at the Fountain Hills Hospice, where she would end up. Emily and Linda followed with briefer and lighter commentary about her ongoing golf competition with her husband. And how she massaged her handicap to get a win every now and then.

Following the service, most people returned to the ranch for drinks and a catered buffet. I spent time with Brian and a few guests, all of whom asked for a comparison with Connecticut. To Brian, I said, "Compared to this, Connecticut is a piece of shit." After that, I talked to the others about the gray weather, traffic congestion, and snow. Finally, Brian and I made plans for a tour tomorrow.

After the guests had left, the girls and I sat around the pool, finishing the margaritas and getting buzzed. Linda left for her office in the home. She spent more time in there than in the corporate office. She said she had work to do, but I thought she just wanted to be alone. Shortly after, Emily needed to go to her shop for a while, an antique store in Fountain Hills. She was also an adjunct faculty member at the Institute of Interior Design. I noticed a change in some of the artifacts in the Great Room. I assumed this was like a floating exhibition for her store. I guessed she also wanted to be alone.

Marilyn and I lay on the double-wide chaise with the cat purring softly on my lap, flexing her toes. We talked about many things, including my return to Connecticut on Saturday. She needed another week to clear up estate matters with the lawyer and her mother's accountant. After that, she planned to sell her car and fly "home." The way she said it relieved my worst fear that she would only say "good-bye" and that would be the end. This gave me a bright new outlook on my… *our* life.

She knew about Charlie, but I hadn't told her about Emma. And she didn't know about my book. So those surprises could wait.

We decided on a nap and another trip to Whiskey Pete's to elevate our mood.

Chapter 15

Brian was picking me up at seven, so I slipped out of bed an hour earlier. I left a softly snoring Marilyn in peaceful sleep, lying on her side with the cat on top of the sheet tucked into the hollow of her bent knees. The rainforest shower felt incredibly refreshing that morning. I thought we all drank too much yesterday.

With my limited wardrobe, I dressed as Southwest as possible and didn't know if I'd look out of place when traveling with Brian. I thought about wearing one of the Stetsons hanging from pegs in the entry. But decided on my Mountainview hat to match the new teal golf polo Marilyn had picked out for me. The mirror showed the beginnings of a rookie tan on my face and arms. Damn, this was the life.

Linda was in the kitchen, sitting at the center island, waiting for the coffee to be ready. She wore a relatively thin nightgown, but didn't seem to take offense at my intrusion (*We're all adults here.*)

I tried to sound as upbeat as I felt when I said, "Another crappy day in Paradise."

"Hey, Dex, what's happening?"

"Brian's picking me up at seven; we're going to tour the area and some of your job sites. Linda, I'm like a kid in a candy store here. Honestly, I'm overwhelmed."

"So, stay Dex, no need to rush home. Stay the damn winter if you want. This is as much Marilyn's house as anyone's." She got up to get the coffee, and I turned to look at the pool.

"I appreciate the offer, but I must go home for several reasons."

"Mar told me she's going to join you as soon as possible. Dex, we hate to see her leave, but we know she's found a good man and a good life. We thank you for that."

"She's brought great joy to my life, Linda. It was pretty empty for a lot of years."

Marilyn came to the door, still in a nightgown but with a colorful blanket wrapped around her. "Morning, folks." The sleepiness was still in her voice, and the cat wrapped around her ankles. "Jesus, Linda, you could have put a robe on."

"Yes, Mommy." Linda held up her empty cup for Marilyn to refill, laughing at her sister's mock embarrassment. She pointed the pot at me, and I waved a no. She put it back on the counter and came to me with a big hug and kiss. I could feel a blush starting and lifted the cup to my lips, unable to say anything. Fortunately, a beeper chirped.

"Driveway alarm; Brian's here," Marilyn announced, then gave me another hug and a goodbye kiss. "Watch out for the burritos and Dos Equis at Tommy and Tito's. That's Brian's idea of a healthy diet." She squeezed my arm and mouthed, "I'll miss you."

***

Brian's Ford F-350 dually came equipped with a large coffee from Dunkin' in the cupholder. "Hey, man," He cheerfully said as he reached a calloused hand across the seat.

"Top o' the mornin' to ye," I tried to put an Irish accent on my greeting to Brian Monahan, "Let's hit it, man, I'm stoked for this."

We drove south into Fountain Hills. Tucked into a high-end shopping mall was Desert Antiques. "That's Emily's place," Brian pointed across the cab.

"Nice place; I guess she does alright with that."

"Yeah, that, and she's a professor at the Interior Design Institute here."

"Nice," I said, swiveling my head back for the last look.

"Yeah, and she's also a lawyer."

"Really?"

"Yeah, she graduated from law school, passed the bar on her first try, and never practiced. I think she just did it as a backup for Big Jim."

"Tell me about him. Big Jim, was he a huge guy?"

"Nah, average-size guy, you've seen the girls. But, big in heart, big in smarts, big in every good way you could imagine. He is one dearly missed sonofabitch. Not just by me, but by the whole community. I could tell you a million stories about how he helped people, and one of them is me. He and Marion were the two closest people I ever met. I think his death started her slide. She just couldn't deal with it. We were lucky to have Linda to grab right on and keep things going.

"This is fascinating, Brian… I don't want to pry, but what can you tell me about Linda?"

"Best damn boss I ever had, except for Big Jim. Smartest, too. She's a Registered Architect and does a lot of our design work, as well as being CEO and running the whole damn thing. Both she and Emily got divorced about five, maybe six years ago, like it was a team decision to dump their husbands. You know, you get to see these girls when they're off-duty and having fun, but let me tell you, they are some serious businessmen." He stopped himself, then laughing, said, "Businesswomen."

I let all this information run around my brain and was about to ask another question when Brian said, "This is our corporate headquarters." He turned toward a two-story adobe-faced building with several other FBC trucks parked under the shade trees at the left of the parking lot.

"I'll just be a minute, Dex; I need to pick up checks for my crew. If I take you inside, all the girls will fuss over Marilyn's boyfriend, and we'll never get out of here." He dashed for the building, leaving the motor and air conditioning running.

When he returned minutes later, two girls came outside to wave as we drove off, heading south to a job site. I waved back, hoping not to look too dorky.

I finally got to ask. "What can you tell me about Marilyn … if you don't mind."

He hesitated, then said, "Well, first thing, we're all pretty damn glad she met you… and let me call you friend." His big hand came across the seat again. We shook, and I knew he meant what he said.

He coughed and said, "Marilyn, she was walking wounded after the crash. I'll tell ya, Dex, we were all pretty damn worried about her, and when she said she was moving to Connecticut, Jesus, I wanted to tie her down. But now we know it was the best damn thing she could'a done… and you're the reason why. God love ya, Dex."

I wasn't sure how to reply. I looked out the side window and wiped my eyes, only managing to squeak out, "Thanks, Brian."

He started again, "I guess I should finish what I started. Marilyn, the oldest, was always assumed to be the CEO after he passed. She's a CPA and handled all the financial shit for Big Jim. But his death affected her the most, and she passed the reins to Linda. So when Jack and Amelia died, she just went to pieces and said she was going as far away as possible. I gotta tell ya, we were pretty damn worried. I still remember the day… what, three years ago, she called Linda and said she was moving in with some guy. I'll tell ya, Dex, if that had been a bad move, I'd have been up there in a heartbeat to take care of things."

I looked at the big hands on the wheel and the forearms the size of my calves and said, laughing nervously, "Thank God you didn't."

He laughed loudly and said, "Don't worry, Dex; you're family now. And we haven't seen Marilyn look this happy in years."

***

We drove another ten miles to a job site with a gorgeous "Rancho Grande" under construction. A catering truck was out front with a crew of guys getting coffee. "Don't worry, Dex, I won't tell them you're a Connecticut liberal." We got out of the truck and approached the men with Brian saying, "This is my good friend, Dex." The crew nodded or saluted a greeting, raising their Styrofoam cups.

***

We had overstuffed burritos and a couple of Dos Equis for lunch. When Brian brought me back to the ranch, Marilyn happily greeted me with a hug and a show-off kiss. "You didn't talk about me, did you, Brian?" She said while keeping an arm around my waist.

"Only the bad stuff, Mar. I tried to warn him," he said with a grin, but I mentally thanked him for the truth. "See ya, Dex… take care."

I was so happy I let that pass, especially when Marilyn turned me around and said, "Pool."

Chapter 16

She was in a playful mood, trying, I was sure, to hide her anxiety about me leaving in the morning. She went into the bathroom to change and I put on the new swimsuit she had bought me while I was out with Brian. It looked much better than the surfer shorts, but now another six inches of white skin was exposed to the Arizona sun.

She came out of the bathroom, also in a new two-piece swimsuit, and began to pose like a Sports Illustrated model. "How do I look, big boy?" And when I made a move at her, she ran out the sliders and across the patio to the pool, shouting, "The last one in is a rotten egg." I hadn't heard that in sixty years. I was right behind her.

Later, the four of us had dinner on the patio. Emily would not let me cook, saying, "Yankees don't know how to treat a good steak." However, she just wanted me to give all my attention to Marilyn on our last night together. Nice thought.

Linda brought out the margaritas and *hors d'oeuvres,* poured drinks for Marilyn and me, and folded up the sunshade so we could sit in the descending glow of a beautiful sunset. We had nothing to do but lie close together on the double chaise and suck up our drinks. I clapped my hands together sharply twice and said, "Refills, chop-chop."

"Yes, Master," Emily said, bowing and scraping with the joke.

As they did on my first night here, the sisters had pressing engagements elsewhere and would not return until after midnight. I think they did that so Marilyn and I could enjoy our privacy.

"Last night," Marilyn said with some sadness, but then turned herself on an elbow, looked straight into my eyes, and continued. "It may be that, Dex, but I honestly feel it's a new beginning for us. I look back on our three years and feel I always kept some barrier between us. I guess, a shield for my insecurity. That's gone now, Dex. You came down here and got a glimpse into my life that I wasn't ready to reveal in Connecticut. I wasn't honest, and I apologize for that. I really do. Can you understand it?"

She hesitated a moment, then continued, "I'm pledging to you complete honesty in our lives going forward. I really want this to work. And I won't let my feelings get in the way. Let's face it, Dex, we're not kids anymore, we're on the down escalator, and we need to get the best out of every day." Finally, she stopped and lay back down, "That's all I've got to say." She reached beside the chaise and got a towel off the deck to wipe her eyes.

I couldn't speak; my mind was in turmoil, and I wasn't sure how to respond. I was hiding the situation with Emma… or whatever her real name was. Playing the fool, I said, "Well, I have a surprise for you when you get home."

"Really?" She was back up on the elbow, looking at me expectantly. "Tell me… c'mon, Dex, tell me." She lowered her voice and put a hand on my white thigh.

"It's supposed to be a secret; this is only a tease."

"You know I'll get it out of you." Her hand began to move.

"Okay, but you can't laugh."

"Tell me!" The hand squeezed.

"I'm writing a novel."

At first, silence. Then she said, "Wow! That's terrific. Tell me more."

"It will be better if I show you when you come home. It's a little hard to explain."

"Okay, but no more secrets."

"Right, no more secrets." I had crossed two fingers like we did as kids.

***

We lay in the purple shadow of the setting sun, which was dropping quickly behind the hills. It was cooler now, and I got a light blanket from the rack in the bedroom. As I spread it over Marilyn, the cat came down off the back of the chaise to make a nest between us, purring softly and kneading. We lay there until it was completely dark except for the pool lights setting a lovely greenish glow in the water. An animal was howling in the distance, probably a coyote.

She lay with her head on my chest, and I was slowly twirling a finger around an errant lock of her hair; she said, "This is nice, but it would be better inside." I took the hint, got up, and helped her to her feet. The cat stayed, content with the full blanket for herself.

After a while, we lay on our backs, holding hands, staring at the unlit ceiling, not saying anything. Finally, I felt the cat jump on the bottom of the bed, then walk the sheet-covered alley between us to the pillows. She bumped us with her head purring into our faces. Getting no response, she retreated to a spot between our feet and settled in for the night, trusting.

***

The clock was set for six, but I woke up ten minutes earlier. As I turned to release the alarm, Marilyn stirred and spoke with a sleep-husky voice, "I've gotta go." She slipped into her pajama boxers, which were on the floor beside the bed, and crossed to the bathroom with arms folded across her naked chest. I arose, put on my sweatpants, and padded into the guest bathroom. When I returned, I heard the shower running and thought there might be an invitation for a minute, but I decided against it. Instead, I grabbed last night's t-shirt and walked across the patio to the kitchen. My bare feet were now accustomed to the stone floor.

Linda had made coffee and was already drinking it as she sat at the island, wearing a bathrobe. She held the cup in both hands, so the steam rose into her nose. Then, finally, she mumbled, "Hi."

"Hi, yourself. You don't look so good."

"I feel like I've been shot at and missed, shit at and hit." She swallowed some coffee and looked at me, not expecting a reply.

I filled a cup and sat down across from her.

"So, where's *Miss I've Got A Boyfriend And You Don't?*" Linda sing-songed that jibe at her sister and then chuckled about it. "Sorry, Dex, you guys missed a good party last night."

Before she could say more, Marilyn entered the room and said, "What makes you think we didn't have a better party because I've got a boyfriend, and you don't."

How could I not laugh at this? Two middle-aged sisters, closer than peas in a pod, needling each other as the Arizona morning sun began reflecting off the pool into the kitchen. After the laughing and the sister hugs, Marilyn grabbed a coffee, stood behind my chair, her free hand circling the top of my shoulders, and asked her sister, "Where's Em?"

"She stayed at Jeff's to help him clean up after the party… and whatever." I felt like the observer of an adult reality show.

Marilyn read me like a book. "Jeff's been her guy for about two years. Great guy: you'll have to meet him when we come back. He's an administrator with the BLM."

I questioned, "BLM?"

"Bureau of Land Management, he's in charge of the mustang program. These beautiful animals he's trying to save with a small budget and a lot of opposition… it's so sad." She dropped her head a little and pressed the cup to her lips.

Linda changed the subject quickly. "What time is your flight, Dex?"

I gave her the flight details, adding, "I sincerely thank you guys for the most beautiful time of my life. I mean it."

Marilyn squeezed my shoulder as Linda said, "You can only thank us by coming back again. You're family now." We drank our coffee after that, and I offered to cook an omelet. No takers.

***

At the airport, Marilyn went as far as the security stop with me, holding my hand in a tight grip. I asked her what she'd do later, and she looked up at me, saying,

"I'm going from here to the driving range at the club and beat the shit out of golf balls 'till my arms fall off."

We hugged and kissed one more time before I got in line. When I looked back, she gave a half-wave and then mouthed, "Take care," with a sly grin.

Chapter 17

There was no severe weather on the return, but our connecting flight to Chicago was delayed two hours. I wanted to call Tom and get the latest news on the "Emma" situation. Still, I couldn't bring myself to do so, as if Marilyn were looking over my shoulder. By the time I arrived in Hartford, it was too late. I would do it tomorrow.

I had brought a warm coat for the flight home and took the shuttle to the parking lot, but I was frozen when I got the car unlocked and the bags inside. When I got home, Tom's note was on the kitchen table.

I came by at 6 and turned up the thermostat. Set the temp at 70. Emma is going to Meadowbrook on Monday. Call me when you unwind.

I read the note twice, got a beer from the fridge, and sat in my winter coat, letting thoughts run free, but the little bastards kept coming back to haunt me... how would I explain this to Marilyn?

***

When I awoke Sunday morning, I thought Marilyn had left the bed. I lay there thinking of her and Arizona and Emma. It was 8:21 a.m.; too early to call Tom, especially since he and Mary Ellen alternated weekends between here and her place on the Lower Cape. I didn't know where he was today.

Back to the oatmeal, as though I had never left. I added raisins and sprinkled some cinnamon on top, more just for something to do than taste. I checked the time; the microwave digital readout was 9:52 a.m., which was close enough. I hit my contacts for *TOM B.*

"Hey, Dex, glad to be back?"

"No!"

"Well, that seems pretty damn definite."

"Look at it this way, Tom. Would you be glad to come back if you were in Paradise with a beautiful, sexy woman you were madly in love with?"

"That good, huh?"

"That good and more, wait 'till I give you the whole story. But, right now, what about Emma?"

"She's been accepted into the Meadowbrook program; Marty's a friend of the Administrator, Dr. Sylvia Englund."

"Is there anybody he doesn't know?"

"Not many… anyway, Emma will be going there tomorrow. I'll be out of town, so Marty and a woman from his office are picking her up at St. Martin's and taking her there. The woman went shopping with Emma yesterday to get her the clothes she'll need. They have a dress code and a lot of rules. But she wants this badly, Dex. So, this is a plus because, as an adult, she's not under court order and could walk out of there Monday afternoon, and we couldn't stop her. And, by the way, your deposit would disappear similarly."

"I'm not worried about that."

"I didn't think so. But it's a pretty big nut to put someone there for eight or ten weeks."

"Okay, what do I do next?"

"Call Dr. Englund for your interview, she'll meet you, and there are papers to sign. Marty's got you covered. He figured that dinner he got out of you last year after you lost the Super Bowl bet was expensive enough to be considered a retainer. So, he told Dr. Englund you were his client."

"Why can't I take her there?"

"Here's the fascinating part. She doesn't want to see you until… and these are her words… she *has her shit together.* Emma's very embarrassed about what happened between you guys. So, Dex, please tell me nothing happened."

"Nothing happened, trust me, Tom. Nothing even remotely happened. I'll tell you the whole story when I see you."

"Of course, I trust you; I don't think you know how to lie. I'll teach you sometime. Just kidding. Call Doctor Englund. Take care."

Tom closed the call, and I sat there thinking it out. I couldn't call Dr. Englund until tomorrow. With the time difference, it was too early to call Marilyn. So I put on sweats and sneakers, grabbed a ball, and went outside. *Jesus, it's cold.*

I shot around for about twenty minutes with no great enthusiasm. My mother used to say I was *at loose ends*. Finally, I scraped the frost off my car windows, since I had stupidly left it outside last night. I went back into the house, got coffee, and called Marilyn.

We'd been apart for about twenty-two hours, and our new relationship was evident in our voices. She called me *hon'* and *sweetheart* and *dear Dex,* something she had never done before. I called her *Mar*; I wasn't good with endearments. We didn't have much to say, so I just rambled. At one point, she held her phone to the cat so I could hear it purr. Emily shouted a greeting from the background. Mar said she would meet with the attorney in the morning and have a better idea of her schedule after that, and would call me tomorrow night. She closed the call with a kissing sound.

***

I sat in my office chair, swiveling slowly back and forth, facing the window, but not seeing anything. My brain was keeping time with the drumming of a single pencil on the desktop: no particular rhythm, just my left-hand fingers working their will. I was trying to weave a paper clip through my right-hand fingers as a magician would fold over a coin. Nothing worked. I was trying to decide when and how to tell Mar about Emma.

I didn't feel shame or guilt. I had tried to avoid Emma and even ran from the room when she threatened to expose herself. It was sad she thought she had to do that. I had at least a week before Marilyn would return. There would be much more information coming from Meadowbrook that would shed some light on Emma's behavior. And prepare me to say the right things in my revelation to Marilyn.

I ran some opening lines, speaking out loud to an empty chair.

"Hi, Marilyn; guess what?...Hey Marilyn, you'll never guess… Marilyn, sit down for a minute. I want to tell you…"

I threw the pencil at a chair cushion like a dart. It bounced off and fell on the floor. I'd talk to Dr. Englund tomorrow, and of course, Tom.

Being alone today, I thought, should be an excellent opportunity to be productive on the book. I had previously punched holes in the narrative pages and placed them chronologically in a three-ring binder. I don't know why thinking about the two women now in my life made me think about my first actual date. I had seen a picture in the box that looked like I was spiffed up to go out with a girl. I was probably thirteen. Fifty-six years later, I was still somewhat embarrassed. I call this:

FIRST KISS

Her name was Maitland, a nice girl, a classmate of mine in 7th grade, and cute. She sat two desks in front of me in homeroom. We had several classes together, met in the halls as we changed rooms, and in the cafeteria at noontime. I probably never would have asked her on a date, so it's good that she asked me.

The only thing unique was that it was my first actual date, and I was pretty nervous. I had never kissed a girl. I practiced in front of a mirror, kissing the back of my hand. I wasn't sure how close that would be. I had been kissed on the lips by my mother when I was a lot younger, but I didn't think that had the same feeling as a puberty kiss on the lips of a cute girl named Maitland.

It wasn't a big-deal date. I met her at her home, waiting outside, and we walked to the Edgewood Cinema for an afternoon showing. I had money from my paper route and bought tickets, popcorn, spearmint leaves, and one large soda with two straws. I figured one drink, two straws, could bring us close together if we both sipped simultaneously. So I was willing to try.

After a while, I put an arm on the back of her seat, and a few minutes later, I tapped her outside shoulder. She turned that way, realized the joke, and we both chuckled. I waited another five minutes and let my hand drop onto her shoulder. She shivered but didn't complain or ask me to move it. When the circulation stopped, and my arm became numb, I brought it back and shared the armrest with her, and we held hands. I couldn't feel anything; my arm was numb, but just the thought of her hand in mine was enough.

It was mid-October, and the sun dropped away early enough that it was nearly dark when the film was over. She told me her mom had baked cookies and would make hot chocolate for us. I think this was just to get us home earlier so Mom could see if any damage had been done.

Three blocks from her house, I began to tense up. The thought of a kiss was quite overwhelming. Truthfully, I was scared shitless. Two blocks, and I was running through my mirror training, trying to mentally warm up like a pitcher in the bullpen. Three houses away, there was a burned-out streetlight, and the darkness covered us like a blanket. I stopped, turned her toward me, put my hands on her upper arms, brought our lips together, kissed, and said, "There!" Almost sixty years later, I still can't believe I was such a dork. I could go to that exact spot, even today.

Chapter 18

Monday morning, my first thought was to call Dr. Englund. It was 7:15 a.m.; that was not going to work. 5:15 a.m. in Arizona, nope. Emma, of course not, and I knew Tom was a late sleeper.

So, I made oatmeal. Then I watched the morning news shows, took a shower, shaved, and cut myself. First, I dressed in what I pictured was appropriate garb for a meeting with a private school administrator. Then, I took most of that off and put on a hoodie and sneakers to shoot some hoops. At 9:30, I figured it was the perfect time and cranked up my phone.

"Meadowbrook Academy, hold, please."

"Crap."

"Meadowbrook Academy, how may I direct your call?"

"Doctor Englund, please. It's Dexter Phillips calling regarding a new client… student."

"Doctor Englund is finishing a call now, please hold, and she'll be right with you."

I held.

A lovely voice came on the line, cheery without being sappy, direct without overbearing. "Good morning, Mr. Phillips; I've been expecting your call. Attorney Kaspersky said you and your wife were in Arizona; how lovely. Now, we need to talk about Miss Spector."

I let one small detail slide and said, "Yes, I know her as Emma, although I understand that is not her real name. Unfortunately, I'm somewhat out of touch with her present situation, which happened while I was away. The only information I have is from Tom Brandt. He said I need to meet with you… papers to sign or something… and I will pay all the bills."

"That is true, we need to meet, and I would like to do that today. I prefer not to meet on campus because Emma is currently reluctant to see you. I can explain that more fully when we meet. So, instead of my office, I'll meet you at Gloria's Tea Shoppe — with two p's — in the village. We can do that today, one thirty?"

Holy shit! And Tom thought the nuns were strict.

I arrived in the village ten past one, not daring to be late. The academy campus could be seen to the west, spreading itself on a hillside with old and historical buildings. Their website told me the girls were housed eight to a "cottage," along with an experienced female counselor. Each cottage was self-contained with kitchens where the girls learned cooking skills. In addition, there was a hybrid library, meeting, and lesson room, where the girls received academic instruction from different subject tutors. Also, two buildings housed the labs and classrooms for a fully accredited high school education. The girls were responsible for managing their cottages under the guidance of the counselors. They planned their menus, duties, and housekeeping as part of developing their life skills. Five cottages were for girls aged fourteen to sixteen years old and three cottages were for those older than sixteen. From the website, I learned that someone of Emma's age and having obtained a GED would receive more advanced instruction to prepare her for possible college entry.

I wish I could be a fly on the wall to see how she was doing, but that was impossible now.

Gloria's was what I expected from a village *shoppe* spelled with two p's. It was quaint. I sat at a small table with a checkered tablecloth near the rear, watching for Dr. Englund. She wasn't hard to spot. A tall woman with a stiff bearing, an open Burberry raincoat, Talbots catalog clothes, and dark-framed glasses hanging on a neck chain. She came through the door as though bringing news of good tidings. The girl serving tea said, "Hi, Doctor Englund."

I rose from my chair and said, "Hello, Doctor Englund," offering my hand.

"Call me Sylvia," She said, shaking hands, sat, put her briefcase on the floor, then said, "My God, what a day." I liked her immediately.

She gave me what information she could and showed me a picture that had been taken as she left the campus of Emma talking with another girl. Emma was looking away. I could not see her face, but she was dressed in a gray pleated skirt and a dark green blazer.

As if reading my mind, she said, "We have a dress code here, and how positively that impacts these girls is incredible. So many of our girls come from harsh circumstances where they probably would have beat up some kid wearing clothes like this. Still, they accept it here as another way of changing their lives. Then, of course, we have a *sloppy Saturday* when they can wear whatever they want. But after a week or two, they begin to moderate away from the bizarre. We also require that any tattoos are covered, and no piercings other than a single set of discreet earrings are allowed. It amazes me the way these kids disfigure their bodies, but that was then, and this is now. So, what do you think, Mr. Phillips?"

I shook my head and blinked before answering. "I'm quite overwhelmed, I went to your website, but I had no idea. So, of course, we are wondering how well Emma will fit in… I know that's not her real name. And please call me Dex."

Before answering, the waitress brought the tea service, and I smelled an herbal aroma. She placed two small menus on the table.

"Emma is the name she has chosen for herself at this point in her life." Sylvia stopped and quickly poured the tea, showing this was not the first time. "She wants a new beginning, and the name change is part of this transition. We have no problem with that; it's quite common here. In fact, some of the girls have their names legally changed. Shall we order?"

After the waitress had taken our order, Sylvia started with, "I can understand you are disappointed in not meeting with her today. I spoke with her about that in our first interview this morning. She is, frankly, embarrassed by some contact she has had with you. But nevertheless, she wants to establish her *new life*," she emphasized with air quotes, "and meet with you. We understand that, and it is quite common in these circumstances. Do you understand, Dex?"

"I do, we want the best for her, and she has our understanding and trust."

"That's good; confidence is everything. Now, I must ask you… did you have any physical contact with this girl?" She leaned forward, arms on the table, eyes boring into me like a rock drill.

I thought, *why doesn't she just hit me with something?* Thank God I didn't have to lie. I looked her straight in the eye and said, "I had no physical contact with this woman." If only Bill Clinton could have been so sure.

"Good, I trust you. Attorney Kaspersky has vouched for you, which goes a long way in my book. Let's talk a little bit about how you and your wife…."

"Oh, I'm sorry there's some misunderstanding here," I started, beginning to feel better with the truth, "Marilyn is my partner. We've been together for over three years now. We're both widowed and have no children. However, Marilyn did have a daughter who was killed, along with her husband, in a traffic accident five years ago when the daughter was fourteen. Marilyn knows teenage daughters."

"I see, and what's her take on this situation?"

"Well, everything has happened so fast while we were in Arizona, along with her mother's passing two weeks ago, the funeral and the estate's settlement. Marilyn, as a CPA, is quite involved down there for the next week or so and —"

"Dex, don't bullshit me. She doesn't know, does she?"

"Not exactly."

At that moment, Sylvia put down her cup and laughed more heartily than I would expect. She wiped her mouth with the cloth napkin and said, "Dex, just tell me the truth. Please know I deal with a dozen or more young ladies blowing smoke at me daily." She laughed again.

I choked a little and said, "You got me. I haven't told Marilyn about this. I'll do so when she comes home; I don't want to do it by phone. Please don't hold this against Emma."

"You're fine if Marty says you're okay; that's good enough for me. The rest of this inquisition is merely the paperwork." She lifted the briefcase onto the table and took out a two-page printed application along with a schedule of rates for the various programs and activities, none of which were cheap. The waitress brought our sandwiches, which were daintily cut, corner to corner.

We ate in silence, which I was grateful for, then, fortified by the dainty tea sandwich, I had the temerity to ask, "What is your background in this field, if I may ask?"

"Of course, you can ask… I was a punk kid who quit school at seventeen and joined the Marines. My last assignment was training female recruits at Parris Island. The Marines were my Meadowbrook." She stopped, lifted the cup, and took a sip, staring at me over the top of the cup and said, "I got a GED and took several college courses during those four years, so I could start as a sophomore when I was discharged. A little bit older, but a whole lot wiser." She laughed a little, put the cup down, and continued, "I worked my butt off taking extra credits and got my bachelor's from UVA in five semesters. Then I returned to New England and got my master's and PhD at UConn. I'm originally from the New Haven area."

"Wow!" I said, picking up my cup and saluting her with it. "I'm impressed."

"Don't be. I got lucky, and I got the G.I. Bill. Be more impressed by a kid like Emma trying to redo a life."

I thought about that and said, "Well, I guess I will be Emma's, G.I. Bill."

"Nicely put, Dex; let's hope it all works out. However, you need to remember this: unless these girls are here under court order, they can walk out of here when they're eighteen, and many do."

She let that sink in for a minute. Then added, "Mr. Brandt paid for the first month with his check. He informed me that they were your funds and that you would be financially responsible going forward."

I exhaled and looked straight at her, "So, we're good. I don't have to go sit in the corner or something?"

"We're good, Dex, we're good." She paid for the tea and signed the check. She stood up, meeting over, "I'll be in touch regarding your visit, and I hope to meet Marilyn at that time. Please mail the application tomorrow."

We shook hands, and she left, nodding to a person I assumed was Gloria. I didn't know if she had included a tip, so I slipped a twenty under the edge of my plate.

I blew out some air and relaxed my shoulders. Nodded to "Gloria" too, and went out the door feeling like I had just been released from the principal's office.

Chapter 19

As I left the village, I pulled over onto a cleared spot at the side of the road, shut off the motor, put my head back against the seat, and tried to clear my brain. This was a significant undertaking; it was more than just writing a check. To be responsible for the well-being of this girl was suddenly overwhelming.

I needed Marilyn. I knew she would welcome Emma… at least, I thought she would. I wanted to call her right now and took out my phone. Fortunately, "Rational Dex" prevailed over "Impulsive Dex." I put the phone away and concentrated on how I would break the news when she returned.

I took out the phone again, called Tom, got his voicemail, and said, "We need to talk. How 'bout bowling and beers? I'm buying, see if Dicky can come. Call me."

***

There was a lot more traffic on the way home. The slow going gave me more time to order my thoughts and work out a game plan. Short-term bowling and beer. Long-term, a commitment to the well-being of a teenage girl. I knew Marilyn will support this. I knew it. Tom called.

"I'm driving, can't talk. Are we on for tonight?"

"Yeah, Dicky, too."

"See ya there at eight o'clock." I shut off the phone and tossed it on the other seat. I hated to use it if I was driving, and I usually didn't, but I was stuck in a parking lot. Probably because some idiot talked on his phone and crashed his car.

***

I put water on for tea, then shut that off and grabbed a beer. I was holding the Meadowbrook application as though it would come alive and bite me. I went to my office, sat, and gave it a quick once-over. It seemed reasonable, and I didn't see it as intrusive. Wishing the print had been a little larger, I made a working copy and began my soulful confession with a pencil. Near the end of the first page, my phone came alive with a call from *MARILYN.*

"Hey, how's it going down there?"

"It's 86 degrees, and I'm sunning topless by the pool."

"Don't move; I'll be right down." She started giggling while I laughed nervously at her little joke.

"I'm just leaving the attorney's office, and I've got good news."

"Great! Tell me."

"It seems we can wrap this up by Thursday. I've booked a flight for Friday afternoon. So, we'll be in each other's arms before midnight. What do you think of that, Big Guy?"

"Keyword, big."

As I laughed, "She said, "Don't overestimate yourself. I'd say more like a medium."

We both laughed at our awkward sex talk, knowing whatever happened when we met would have old-age limitations. "I, honest to God, can't wait Mar. It's been pretty lonely here."

"I'm the same, Dex, and I've got my sisters and this spectacular environment. Of course, the estate closing will keep me busy, but I'm missing something, too. I'm missing you, Dex."

I could feel she was getting teary, and although it made me feel kind of special, I didn't want to stress her out, so I said, "Hey, I've got some water boiling over... send me your flight details by text... I've got to get this... I'll call you later."

I killed the phone and stood there in the spotlight of my stupidity. A reasonable person would have walked into the kitchen with the cell phone and shut off the stove. I'd call her later.

Cleaning up after my meal, I began to feel uneasy about our future. What if Marilyn couldn't accept my involvement with Emma, as innocent in motive as that was?

What the hell *was* my motive? I thought about it and couldn't answer in thirty words or less. I dried my hands and sat at the kitchen table with a cup of tea, considering this was how it all started. Thinking about this young woman… girl, who had come to my house on what I had assumed was a pretext… but for what? I wasn't especially attractive, especially to someone young, sweet, and outgoing. I was more in the old, crusty, and noncommittal category. I remembered giving her that box of candy at Staples. Was that enough for me to be her knight in shining armor? *If so*, I thought, *that is sorrowful, and she is so vulnerable.*

I remember the many years when Barbara and I thought we could be parents. Why not? Everyone else was. Then our selfish refusal to bring an adopted life into our family. Was that what I was feeling — guilt? I didn't know.

I had an hour to wait before leaving for the bowling alley, and assumed Marilyn would be back at the ranch by now. But, of course, that was the ranch, and here in Connecticut was "home," as she'd said. So I got her voicemail and left a fast-talking, rambling message.

"Hey, sorry I had to run for the kettle before. How stupid of me to hang up. I don't mean, *hang up*, you know what I'm saying. And I didn't get a chance to say — I love you. Imagine that. Wow, was that a dumb thing to say… I don't mean love. I mean the part about, imagine that. I'm rambling like an idiot… I guess that's because I miss you so much. And I haven't eaten in days… just kidding… about the eating. I just had dinner. I love you. I will take my foot out of my mouth and call you again later. I'm going bowling with Tom and Dicky, the league starts Wednesday. Happy trails… how's that for Southwest lingo? I really do love you."

I put the phone on the table and stared at it as if it were at fault.

***

I finished the final frame conquering a 7-10 split, which, in our trio of happy bowlers, earned me a lot of grumbling and five bucks each from Tom and Dicky.

We usually sat at the bar but tonight, I wanted to speak more quietly with them, so we got a booth at the back of the restaurant. In some respects, Tom knew more about this situation than I did. It was all new to Dick Doc, who listened intently to my Emma tale, not questioning until I had finished and signaled to Jennifer for another round.

"Jesus, Dex, that's quite a story. Does Marilyn know?"

"Thanks, Dick, stab me in the back again. No, she doesn't. She knows something's going on. I had to tell her there was a little surprise when she came home. I didn't want to do that, but she reads me like a damn book. So I had to tell her something."

Dicky continued his inquisition while Tom just sat there without any sympathy. "What are you going to say?"

I put my beer down and spoke to his face. "That's what the hell you guys are supposed to help me with."

"Sorry, Dex, I'm an eye guy; you need a psychiatrist, or better yet, a proctologist to help you get your head out of your ass." He and Tom convulsed in laughter. I beaned him with a rolled-up napkin, "Fuckers!"

***

I didn't get much sympathy or advice from my friends, so I rehearsed my next call on the way home. As soon as I got in the house, I went to the chair without removing my coat, pulled out my phone, and called. It was only 9:40 in Arizona.

"Hi, sweetheart. Is everything okay?"

"You bet, Mar, couldn't be better, four hours closer to being together."

"Four hours and ten minutes, but who's counting." She laughed, then said, "Is everything alright there?"

"Sure, why not?"

"Because I know you, Dex. What's going on?"

"Nothing… really."

"Don't lie to me, Dex; your nose will grow."

"Very funny; I was thinking about the surprise I have for you."

"And you're not going to tell me."

"And you're not here to make me. There!" I said, as I thought about *THE FIRST KISS.*

She laughed and said, "You're impossible… hold on, my sisters both say hello."

"Hello, back at them. Hey, did you get a cat carrier?" *Good distraction, Dex.*

"I bought one at the airport after you left. It's an official Southwest Airlines kitty carrier. It probably cost twice what one would at Walmart, but I thought she'd get special treatment if she was official. And I bought an absorbent pad in case she has an accident. She's going to be right with me, under the seat."

"That's good. Did you sell your car?"

"I did; I took it to Carmax, and they checked it thoroughly and gave me a check right there. Linda picked me up; I've been using the Chrysler since then."

"Great, shopping for a new car together will be fun."

"It will, Dex, and if you don't stop bullshitting me about your surprise, I'm going shopping for a new man. Nighty-night, kiss, kiss." Call ended.

Damn, she sees right through me. At least she didn't say "take care."

Chapter 20

The next three days went as expected; calls back and forth with my sweetheart. Fun on the phone. We were both in a good mood. I never thought two older people could act so silly. It was great. I know she was waiting for me to cave on the surprise, but I stayed strong. We talked about the cat and other safe topics until the last night when she said, "Well."

"Well, what?"

"Are you going to tell me?"

"When you come home. It's like a surprise magnet; it ensures your return."

"It had better be good."

***

Predictably, her flight connection was delayed at O'Hare, and she arrived in Hartford just after midnight. We hugged, kissed, the usual stuff, and I ran my hand across the cat carrier door. She seemed to be in shock inside her little cage.

There was a short wait for her baggage, and Marilyn cuddled herself in the full-length winter down coat and hood I had brought home. She pressed against me as if I could provide additional warmth. When I got the bags, she waited inside the terminal while I ran for the car. "Jesus, it's cold."

We didn't say much until I hit the interstate and she had warmed up. She told me about the estate settlement and that Emily and Jeff might get engaged. Linda had gone to Hawaii with a new friend, and Brian said, "Hello."

I talked about bowling, cleaning the house, and the suddenly cold weather, but nothing about Emma. I didn't realize Marilyn had fallen asleep.

***

When we got home, I pulled up at the back door. Before Marilyn got out, she said, "Do you mind if I sleep in my own bed tonight? I'm so exhausted, I won't be good company."

"Of course, you go right up. What can I bring you… tea?"

"Would you mind making a hot chocolate?"

She got out before I could answer. I watched her climb the stairs, holding the railing in one hand and the cat carrier in the other as she climbed the three porch stairs in utter exhaustion. It must have been a stressful week for her.

When I brought her luggage in, she was holding the vase of flowers I had bought earlier, smelling the aromas. "They're beautiful, Dex, thank you." The cat was hunched over the dry kibble I had put in her place before I left for the airport. Marilyn went upstairs while I parked the car in the garage and got started on her hot chocolate.

Trying not to scald the milk, I kept stirring until there was a hint of steam, tested a spoonful, and poured her a mug. When I got upstairs, she was in bed with the covers to her chin, fast asleep. I moved her travel clothes off the chair and sat there, sipping the hot chocolate and thinking I was the luckiest guy in the world. The cat walked the length of her body before curling up at her feet.

***

The next morning, I wanted to serve her breakfast in bed, but didn't want to wake her, so I went to my office to fool around with some notes for the book. When I heard her steps coming downstairs, I decided on a little joke and pretended I didn't hear her approach. Suddenly, something dropped in my lap. An angry voice behind me screamed, "I hope you enjoyed it! You sick fuck!"

I swiveled around with a pair of skimpy lace panties in my lap, staring at Marilyn's back as she headed for the door shouting, "I'm leaving!"

I was angry. "You come back here and sit down!" I shouted, and I think the timbre of my voice was so unexpected that it stopped her in the doorway. She turned. I calmed down a little and said, "Please, Mar, please sit down; let me tell you about this. It's all good, Mar, honest, it's all good, trust me. You must hear the whole story… please, sit down, please." I gestured to the ladder-back cane seat chair at the side of my desk. She stared at me with a face I had never seen before, but pulled the chair away about three feet and sat, fists clenched, eyes on fire.

I began by saying, "Please let me tell you everything before you ask any questions, and you can verify everything by calling Tom." She still looked skeptical, but at least was willing to hear me out.

I began with the chair and Staples and the box of candy. Then, I went on to the warranty, the herbal tea, the market, the Post Office, and finally, Emma breaking in and me finding her in the bed. I told her everything; I had no reason to lie.

I told her about Tom, the trespass, the cops, and St. Martin's. About Emma's family and her record, Meadowbrook and Dr. Englund. I spoke rapidly, not wasting a breath, not holding anything back.

When I finished, I said, "Call Tom, ask him anything. Marty and one of the women from his office were involved, too." I was breathing heavily, spent by my oratory, hoping I got through to her.

She started with small tears leaking out the corners of her eyes, her face crumbling, and her shoulders shaking. She put her hands over her mouth, and the eyes above them stared at me like a frightened child. Finally, she started to speak, and her world collapsed. She reached out her arms, still sitting, and I swiveled my chair toward her, bringing those hands to my lips.

I stood up, lifting her to her feet, and she collapsed into my arms. I believed she would have fallen if I were not there. But, instead, her tears began to soak my skin, her face buried in my bathrobe. She tried to speak but kept choking on her words until I thought I heard her say, "Amelia."

Time didn't mean anything. I wasn't sure how long we stood there. Even after the crying stopped, she held me as if I were the lifebuoy for a drowning person. Finally, I helped her into the living room, sat her on the couch, and covered her with the afghan, tucking it under her bare feet. She hugged a throw pillow to her chest and buried her face in it.

"Can I get you some tea?"

"Would you make me a hot chocolate, please?" The words were like a child's, mumbled through the pillow; she did not look up.

"I'm going to draw a hot bath for you," I said while brushing her hair back from her face.

"Thank you, sweet Dex; I'm so sorry." But unfortunately, she still didn't look up.

I started water in the bath, then put milk on the stove for the chocolate, stirred it to a near-boil, filled a large mug, and put in a dollop of Marshmallow Fluff, one of her little tricks. She took the mug in both hands and looked at me with brighter eyes and a soft voice saying, "When can I meet her?"

"I'll call Dr. Englund after nine and schedule a visit. Also, I'm not sure Emma is ready to meet us. I hope so."

"Make it happen, Dex," She implored. "Please make it happen." She stood up and gripped my arm with surprising strength. "I'm going upstairs. Come up in a little while." She kissed my cheek.

***

When I entered the bathroom, she was swaddled in bath bubbles, showing only her face and bent knees. I sat on the tub's edge, and she placed a hand over mine. It wasn't a time to say anything. We just looked at each other and felt closer than ever before. Finally, she told me about an Apache legend that says, *If a child dies before becoming an adult, that child will reappear as another person in the lives of that family*. She closed her eyes and whispered, "Amelia." I wiped my eyes on my bathrobe sleeve.

***

The closeness we felt in the bed after that was more than ever. We were about to share something special. We were unsure how Emma would feel, but we both wanted to call it a family. Shortly after nine, I called Dr. Englund with Marilyn curled in my arm. I could feel Marilyn's tension as I spoke.

It was a yes, and Marilyn squeezed my arm. Dr. Englund had already spoken with Emma about a possible visit today, telling her that I would meet with Emma first so that whatever she felt a need to apologize for could be resolved. During that time, Dr. Englund would chat with Marilyn. Then, finally, the three of us would get together as one big happy family and eventually be joined by Dr. Englund.

"Also, Mr. Phillips, Emma, has asked that she be allowed to take piano lessons. Ms. Greer has auditioned her and has high praise; hoping you will allow that. The lesson charge is listed on the schedule I gave you Monday."

"Go for it." That was a quick response, but I was so happy I didn't know what I was saying.

When I finished the call, Marilyn kissed me hard. Then, she got up to go dress, throwing a towel across her naked shoulders. She swayed her hips in happily exaggerated movement as she left my room. She stopped at the door and again said, "I'm really sorry, Dex, I was a real bitch."

***

I searched my closet for as tweedy an outfit as possible, finally settling on dark green cords, a Harris tweed sports coat, a black turtleneck, and boat shoes. I approved of myself in the mirror.

I was waiting in the living room when Marilyn came downstairs. I'd never seen her look so beautiful. Her hair was cut before leaving Arizona, now curled under just above her shoulders. She wore a wool pantsuit and a white oxford button-down shirt, complete with a small black bowtie-like accessory with a tiny gold clasp. A single strand of pearls was around her neck, and several thin gold bracelets encircled her left wrist. The shoes also looked new, with a two-inch heel that brought her eyes even to my shoulder. She had applied makeup with artistry that was new to me and carried a subtle perfume scent that I liked but couldn't name.

"Wow! You're a knockout."

"Thank you, hon', you're not so bad yourself. I'd kiss you all over your face except for the lipstick… but the thought is there." She laughed.

***

What did I do to deserve a day like this? Beautiful, bright weather, not too cold for early November. Light traffic, my woman at my side humming some little melody I didn't know, full of excitement to meet Emma.

Marilyn was in high spirits. "Damn good surprise, Dex; maybe I'll surprise you with something special tonight."

"Promises, promises."

We both laughed like idiots, and then I broke out in a loud, off-key chorus of *Oh, Susannah.* We were still singing as I pulled into the postcard-perfect campus of Meadowbrook Academy.

The administration building was at the center of a tree-lined village green. It was previously a headquarters building for the Patriot army during the Revolutionary War. Most of the buildings were built in the 18th century. Two new buildings looked like a gymnasium and a lab. It was historical and stunning.

We had to wait a few minutes in the reception before Dr. Sylvia Englund could see us. Then, finally, she opened her door and greeted us like old friends, shaking our hands. Next, she directed us to sit — not at her desk, but on sofas beside a glowing fireplace at the side of her office. "Would you care for coffee? I'd love some."

We both agreed that would be nice. Minutes later, with no apparent summons from Sylvia, the door opened, and the woman from the reception wheeled in a serving cart.

After the coffee, in her subtle manner, Sylvia said, "Dex, Emma, is ready to see you now. But, first, I hope you will accept her apology for whatever she feels wrong about. I have a fair idea, but I'm leaving that responsibility to her."

She turned to Marilyn and, in no less of an abrupt manner, said, "May I call you Marilyn?" Then, without waiting for a reply, she added, "While Dex is with her, you and I will chat. We also have a form for you to take back with you. Please fill that out and mail it back on Monday; thank you."

I was watching some concern wash over Marilyn's face. Then I watched it disappear when Sylvia added, "Please excuse my brusque manner. I had a really pissy day before you got here." We all chuckled at that.

"Okay, Dex, let's take a little walk. Marilyn, please make yourself comfortable, and have more coffee. If there's anything else you need, Sally at the reception desk will take care of you. My bathroom is behind that door." She said, pointing to a paneled wood door behind her desk. "C'mon, Dex, let's go."

I felt like I'd been given marching orders. We strolled down the green approaching the cottages. It was pleasantly warm, and my sport coat was adequate. Emma was sitting on a bench ahead. Sylvia said, "I like to see these meetings happen outdoors. It gives everybody a better chance to speak and act more freely. And we couldn't have a nicer day. I only wish I could have a cigarette." The young woman turned toward us when we were about twenty feet from the bench. Sylvia said, "I'll leave you two alone; both of you come to my office when you're ready."

Emma stood up, smiling, but I knew she was uneasy and looked ready to bolt. I wet my lips and tried to speak, only squeaking, "Emma, oh dear God, Emma." I approached with a hand extended. She stood and grasped that and put her other hand on top. She had red-rimmed eyes and a sniffle that she wiped with her left sleeve as she released my hand.

"Mr. Phil… Dex, I don't know where to start. First, I need to apologize, big time, for what I've done. I think I was stalking you. Can you believe that?"

She hesitated, but I didn't think she expected an answer. "You gave me a little box of malt balls at Staples. Do you remember?" I nodded. "That meant a lot to me, Dex; you gave that to me because you wanted to, expecting nothing in return. I could have mailed the warranty, but I needed to meet a *good guy* again," she framed that in air quotes. "I haven't met too many *good guys* in my life, especially around my age. They're all looking for something back. I wanted someone to, you know, just be with someone I could trust. Then I got out of control. I don't do drugs, Dex, I saw what it did to my mother, and I don't want any piece of that. But, somehow, I got out of control."

She was starting to tear up, so I said, "Let's walk a little," And put my arm around her shoulders. I guessed this is what fathers and daughters could do. So we walked out on the green.

Then stopped, and she turned to me saying, "Dex, I was a real shit, I mean a *real* shit, trespassing into your house and that crazy scene on the bed, and you were so… what do I want to say… so good, you ran from the room. I guess I was lucky; not many guys would have done that."

"But, Dex, what I really feel sorry about, I mean it, I hate myself for what I did, putting my panties under your wife's… girlfriend's pillow. That was pretty damn stupid, and I hope you and your girlfriend will forgive me… please forgive me." She took some tissue out of her blazer pocket and wiped her eyes. We walked on without talking but turned back toward the administration building. I sensed that we were coming to an end.

She was a tough kid. She got herself under control, stopped, looked up at me, and said with a sincerity that overwhelmed me, "I'll make you proud. I know this is expensive, and I can't say how much I appreciate it. I'm not going to say I'll pay you back, because I probably will never be able to do that. The only thing I can do is make you proud… I *will* do that." She stuck out her hand to seal the deal and shook my hand with a determined strength that made me believe her.

I held her hand a little longer, then said, "I believe you." And I meant it. Then, more upbeat, I said, "C'mon, Marilyn is waiting and probably chewed her fingernails down to the quick by now."

We walked back down the green, arm in arm, with a much lighter step. I summarized my relationship with Marilyn and a little history of the tragic loss of her husband and daughter. I wanted to warn her, so Emma could expect a possible meltdown from Marilyn.

Sylvia had been called out to one of the cottages, so Sally let Emma into the office. I could see Marilyn rise from the couch by the fireplace and approach Emma with open arms. Sally closed the door, but I sat on the bench outside, straining to hear speech through the dense wood panels. I learned later that there had been a lot of tears and a lot of hope — even plans for the Thanksgiving holiday. Emma asked if she could call Mar "Mom," bringing fresh tears and close hugs.

When it was over, two lovely, red-faced, happy women came arm in arm through the door. I stood up, we all hugged, and I heard Emma say, "Family."

As we left the campus, Marilyn said, "I need a drink." When we got in the car, she repaired her make-up damage in the turned-down visor mirror. She stopped and squeezed my arm, saying, "I love her, Dex. Can we be a family?"

Chapter 21

About two miles from campus, the Olde North Taverne appeared on the south side of the road. I always wondered how someone would inscribe a concrete block building using colonial-heritage-type lettering and then get the compass logo direction incorrect.

They had done a better job inside, with a low, beamed ceiling, dark décor, and a massive fieldstone fireplace. It was a cozy spot to unwind. The place was nearly empty mid-afternoon, so we sat at the bar. Not having eaten since breakfast, both of us having been too excited for real food, we attacked the bowl of cheese-flavored snack crackers in front of us. We finished them soon after receiving our drinks. We looked at each other, smiled, raised our glasses, clinked, and toasted, "To family."

I declined a second drink, but Marilyn had another bourbon and soda. She said, "Back in my New England home, out of margarita season," raising her glass in salute. We devoured another bowl of crackers and left. The bartender said, "Thanks, folks hope to see you again," as he pocketed a hefty tip.

In the car, Marilyn said, "We need to stop at Home Depot."

"Oh, what for?"

"Paint chip things, you know, to pick out colors."

"Colors for what?"

"Her bedroom, *jeez Louise*, Dex, we need to spruce up the back bedroom for her. She'll be coming home for four days at Thanksgiving."

I began to see that I would be only a bit player in this drama. I had lived alone for many years and got quite used to that. Then, the time with Marilyn evolved into something unique but still uncertain in my mind. *And, now a teenage girl?* I had to work on this.

Marilyn continued, her voice rising with anticipation, "We only have two weeks to get this done. She'll be coming the Wednesday before Thanksgiving and doesn't have to be back until three o'clock Sunday."

"How did you find this out?"

"Sylvia gave me the schedule. She said it had to be a mutual decision for Emma and us to do this. Only a few of the girls remain over the holiday. Sylvia and her husband take them into their home. The school basically shuts down for that period."

"Okay."

"Okay, what?" Her voice took on a little edge.

"Well, I guess that's what we do."

She turned against the seat belt and leaned a little to look directly into my face. "You don't seem very enthusiastic about this. Is there a problem?"

"No, not a big problem, it's just that we're finally beginning to really know each other, and now there's a new presence to deal with. I guess that's what I mean… I'm selfish, Mar. I feel funny about sharing you."

We drove for several miles in silence; only the road noises kept the car alive. Finally, she said, "I am yours; you are mine. We have an absolute bond. If you want me to pledge to this, I will. I'll do or say whatever you need to feel comfortable with our relationship. I'll marry you if you want; wait for you to ask me, and if you do, I'd be thrilled to say yes. Don't say it now, Dex; you'll know when the time is right."

She stopped, turned away, looked out her side window for a moment, then turned back and said, "Emma is a person we are both involved with now. We can offer her a place of refuge, guidance, love, and a chance for a decent life through your generosity. She's not our progeny; she's more like our friend. I have more of an emotional attachment than you may have because of the loss of my daughter, but that doesn't mean I favor her over you. It's not a competition. Please believe me." She hesitated, looking at me for a reply.

How could four decades flash so quickly through the mind? Suddenly, I was back with Barbara when we made the final decision not to adopt a child into our family. So here was an opportunity to assuage my guilt and do something right. Yes, Marilyn and I were solid; the magic of Arizona had stayed with us and made our relationship more fabulous than ever. I didn't think I was speaking out loud when I challenged myself, "Don't be an asshole, Dex."

"*What?*" Marilyn was looking directly into my eyes, squinting. "What did you say?"

Thankfully, the Home Depot appeared just ahead, and I pointed, saying, "Home Depot."

She looked, and turned back to me about to speak again when I said, "Let me park, and we can talk this out."

We spent about ten minutes baring our souls. In fact, I did all the baring and finally said, "That was almost cathartic. I've been entirely honest with myself for the first time and worked through thirty years of guilt. I do want this to work out… for all of us. Help me through this, Mar; it's a big step. Writing checks is easy; sharing you and sharing our home, not so much."

She unclicked her seatbelt, got partway up onto the seat, and, leaning over, took my face in her hands, kissed me hard, sat back, and said, "I'll get you through it; you won't even know it's happening." She shook her head slowly back and forth, giving me her Cheshire Cat grin. Then said, "Let's get some paint chips."

She couldn't wait to get to the back bedroom when we got home. Ironically, it had been my room for much of my youth. She dropped her coat on a chair and trotted up the stairs with the cat at her heels. I picked up her coat and stood there a minute, breathing deeply. Finally saying to myself, "I can do this."

When I woke the following day, the bed was empty beside me. The sheets were cold. Marilyn must have been up for some time. The clock digits read 5:18. I went downstairs and smiled at the sight of my Marilyn, sitting cross-legged on the couch, robe open over pajamas, a bag of potato chips at her side. A Meadowbrook brochure was on her lap, and the cat stretched across the top of the sofa.

She was breathing softly, head down, completely asleep. I was unsure whether to cover her with an afghan, thinking that might wake her, so I just stood there a moment, trying to time my breathing with hers. The cat sensed my presence, opened her sleepy eyes, and poked at Marilyn's hair with one curved paw. That woke her, and she was startled to see me standing there. "Are you alright?" She managed to say through dry lips.

"Are you kidding? I couldn't be better… or happier… or more in love." I stumbled over the words, but she understood me correctly and held her hands for help standing up.

I helped her up and into my arms, and we stood there swaying slightly while the cat was reaching to bat the undone robe tie hanging at her side. Finally, she said, "I think I need to go back to bed. I was so excited when I woke and figured I'd be restless and wake you, so I came down here. Did you ever eat potato chips at two in the morning?" It wasn't a question that needed an answer. I helped her up, and we went back upstairs with my arm around her waist and the cat running up between our legs.

Later in the morning, armed with a list she had prepared, we went to Home Depot for the needed supplies to recreate the back bedroom and bring it up to snuff for a teenage girl. This really was a lot of fun. And while Marilyn was watching the paint cans vibrating in the mixing machine, I was looking at her and the happy glow that lit her face. I could now see how much this meant to her.

The following two weeks were busy in many ways. The approaching Thanksgiving holiday, the bedroom renovations, and, of course, the anticipation of Emma's visit. This left little time to work on my book. Marilyn was supportive of my efforts. Still, under the circumstances brought to us by Emma, I don't think she was acutely aware of my goal or the process of getting there. I worked on completing the outline, which was beginning to make some sense, but I figured it was a good time to put it away for a while. We had a bedroom to do.

Fortunately, that room had been stripped of wallpaper and the surfaces primed and painted twenty years ago. So the new process was quite simple. My first job was on the ceiling. Marilyn had picked out a new overhead light fixture to replace the one installed when the house was built in the '20s. That made a big difference, especially against the off-white paint I was tall enough to roll on without using a ladder. Next, I rolled soft neutral paint onto the walls. Then, as I expected from an accountant, Marilyn masked around every bit of the woodwork and daintily painted that with a small brush. She was thrilled doing this, looking elf-like in an oversized shirt of mine with her hair stowed under a UConn stocking cap.

The bathroom fixtures, although original, were in perfect condition and gave the small bathroom a bit of antique charm. After painting the walls herself, Marilyn instructed me to put a 6" roll of stencil-looking vinyl fish around the perimeter at the top of the walls. When I suggested this was dorky and would probably come unglued with the shower steam, I got *the look* and a, "Never mind, I'll do it myself" response.

Later that afternoon, while I was removing the last of the masking tape and folding up the drop cloths, she entered the room with an open wine bottle and two glasses. She poured, we clinked, and said, "Thank God, we make a helluva team."

We sat at the foot of the bed, admiring our handiwork and drinking. After the wine, we started kissing, and after that got fully on the bed. Painting could have its own rewards.

Chapter 22

At breakfast on Monday, Marilyn had a pad and pen, making a to-do list for the upcoming holiday. She exhibited childlike enthusiasm for this event. I had never been a big holiday person. With the small family, we didn't do that much when I was a kid.

Marilyn asked, "What about Tom and Mary Ellen? Do you think they'd come? I'd love to ask them. I don't know if they've made any plans."

"Why not? It doesn't hurt to ask, but how might this affect Emma?"

"Dex, she's got to function in the real world, and her previous contact with Tom or Marty is something she's got to learn to face. We can give her love and support, as I've said before, but we can't change history. I think it would be good for her to meet Tom under different circumstances than last time."

"Should I call Sylvia?"

"No, this is between us. We've also got some learning to do, and we can't keep hiding behind Sylvia."

I looked at the time and decided it was too early to call Tom. Still, the more I thought about it, the more it seemed like a great idea to celebrate the holiday with more people.

Marilyn was planning a furniture-buying trip. She had finally convinced me the bedroom furniture, as lovely as it was, was better suited for The Salvation Army, not for a young woman. I kept the chair my mother used at her sewing machine, planning to eventually refinish it.

Marilyn asked if I wanted to go with her, but shopping was not something I had much patience for. I convinced her I'd be a hindrance and better left at home. Besides, I had other plans.

An hour later, I called Tom, and he said he thought Thanksgiving dinner would be a good time; he'd call Mary Ellen and confirm. He expected it would be a go.

I called Party Rental and inquired about renting a suitable table and set of chairs. Speaking with Gwen, who described herself as a *Certified Party Planner* (who knew), I reserved a table with upgraded padded chairs, table covers, a punch bowl, and candlesticks. This woman could sell ice to Eskimos. It took a couple of minutes to catch my breath, then I called Linda at the ranch.

***

I thought Marilyn was excited about redecorating the bedroom. I had no idea furniture buying could be so exhilarating. Instead, she was giddy and came through the back door like Mary Poppins, barely touching the floor. I had just poured the last of the coffee and offered to share, but she said, "Thanks, I'm good… sit down… let me tell you."

Before she continued, I asked, "Jelly donut?"

"What?"

I pointed to the side of my mouth, indicating something was on hers.

She reached it with her tongue and said, "Jelly stick… shut up, let me show you what I got." She proceeded to show me the pictures on her phone of the new furniture. This included a queen-size bed, dresser, blanket chest, and desk, all in white. She said my mother's chair could work at the desk. In addition, there was an upholstered boudoir chair that looked comfortable for reading or napping and a whole shitload of accessories for bed and bath. She'd also bought linens, blankets, curtains, and pillows but had no pictures.

She saw me turning over numbers in my head and said, "Drop it. It's my money," and went into the bathroom.

***

We went out for dinner that night, nothing special, just a chance to get away from the house and get ribs and a pitcher of beer at Applebee's. I told her about Tom and the rented furniture for the holiday.

"Why'd you get a punch bowl?" She mumbled, ripping BBQ pork off a rib bone with her teeth.

"Why not? I might want to make some punch." She thought about that, but didn't reply. I almost slipped up and mentioned the call to Linda.

***

The scheduling worked out great. The Salvation Army would pick up the old stuff Thursday morning, and Framptons would deliver the new furniture that afternoon. We sat there discussing the new look for the room, then realized we had forgotten a rug. The hardwood floors were in good shape, so I planned to wax them, and Marilyn would go back to the store tomorrow for a carpet. Everything was coming together in a hurry.

***

We received an email from Meadowbrook advising that all *parents, guardians, et al.* needed to contact the school no later than Monday of the holiday week to confirm plans for the students in their care. Instead of an email, I decided to call and, hopefully, chat a little about Emma.

There was a brief hold before Sylvia could talk, "I'm glad you called Dex. So many people just email me, and I don't know their feelings behind it."

I felt like I was about to be interrogated. "How's Emma doing?"

"Very well, smart kid… doing well in the college prep courses with her tutors… very well on the piano. Apparently, she was taught some music in a group home when she was younger. Do you have a piano at home?"

"I do; it's my mother's old Knabe studio piano."

"Is it tuned?"

"I don't know, probably not."

"Get it tuned. She'll love it."

I felt the need to stand at attention and mumbled, "Yes. Sir."

"I'm sorry, I didn't hear you."

"I just said I'll get right on it."

"Good, one more thing… she's been elected Cottage Captain for the two weeks when the girls return."

"Is that good?"

"It means that the other girls have elected her to lead them for two weeks. It means they trust her and are confident in her leadership. The captains are elected every two weeks and can be reelected for another two weeks, but that's rare. They basically run the show, with the guidance of the Cottage Counselor, of course. But it's a position with a lot of responsibility, advising and controlling seven of your peers in a close setting, as we have here. So, Dex, what it really says is: this girl is moving on. I like everything I see and hear about her."

I was silent, sucking all that information deep inside, unable to respond.

"You with me, Dex?"

"I am; I'm so thrilled, I couldn't speak. Wait 'till I tell Marilyn."

"Good on both of you, Dex. Remember you have to stop at the office when you come to sign release papers. So if I don't see you, let me wish you a happy holiday now. Take care."

She cut the call before I could wish her the same. I thought she would have been the last person in the world to say, "Take care."

***

Marilyn needed to get her new car. The selection was no problem; she liked mine and wanted the same thing in Oxford White. On the way to rug buying, we stopped at my dealer and got the same salesman and manager I had dealt with. Salesman remembered me and hoped Marilyn would be a little easier to deal with. Fat chance.

Marilyn asked that he not waste her time and wanted his best price now. Salesman deferred to the manager in his glass-cased office and, after their phony deliberation, brought fake smiles and a piece of paper back into the showroom.

"Mrs. Brewer, how nice to meet you." Sales Manager approached with an extended hand, and the paper held slightly behind him as though it were a national secret. They shook hands, Marilyn smiling cordially. "I've worked this number down with Jim," Sales Manager acknowledged the young man at his side with a nod, "And this is our best number on that car. I've wrung out every possible discount I can, and that is our best number, and frankly, we're just about breaking even." At last, he handed her the paper and let the showroom lights highlight his wolf-like smile.

I hung back as Marilyn examined the paper for at least a minute. I watched the nervous feelings revealed by both the salespeople. Finally, she stared hard at the man for a while, eyes slightly squinted, and said, "This is unacceptable."

When she was done with them, a much lower price was accepted, and the car would be ready when we had purchased the rugs. The sales team looked like they needed a bathroom break.

"Jesus, I thought I had some negotiating skills with all my years in retail." We walked across the lot to my car. "But you were unbelievable. Where'd you learn to deal like that?"

"Big Jim."

***

The rugs were no problem. Marilyn knew what she wanted. The car was ready when we got back to the dealer. I drove my car into the driveway first to use the door opener. She parked outside the garage, the motor still running, got out and slowly walked around the car, touching it in several places and saying, "It's nice. I'll keep it." As if there were any indecision, she'd have it back on the dealer's lot in a heartbeat. Big Jim's little girl goes car buying.

The VW Emma drove belonged to some guy she had an "arrangement" with. We didn't like that sound and were relieved when he came to pick it up last week. However, I didn't like his looks and watched from the porch as he drove away. We hoped that was the end of another episode from her past.

Chapter 23

As the holiday neared, we seemed to get more anxious. Amazingly, planning a simple celebration could impact two people who celebrated Thanksgiving in our three years together by going out for dinner and returning home for a nap. Marilyn wanted to make the dinner, along with help from Emma. Apparently, they had discussed this during their meeting in Sylvia's office. I was smart enough not to make any comments regarding the meal or its preparation, and put my efforts into picking up supplies as directed and cleaning the house.

There was no bowling league the night before the holiday, but I bowled my highest score in the previous week. Afterward, at the bar, I had an excellent chance to discuss the Emma situation with Tom, Dicky, and our new member, Russell. He was younger than us and still had one college-aged daughter living at home. I picked up a lot of advice, but with my high score exhilaration, I forgot most of it by morning.

***

I was restless the night before I drove to Meadowbrook. I was unsure what we would say to each other on the trip home. Marilyn decided not to go with me, thinking that would give Emma and me time to work out any kinks in our relationship. I appreciated that.

***

When I stopped at the office to sign the visitation papers, Sally said that Dr. Englund had gone home. Still, she left a sticky note on the form again, wishing us a *Happy Thanksgiving*. That was nice.

Emma must have been watching from inside the cottage. As soon as I parked, she ran out, put her small suitcase on the back seat, and said, "Hi, Dex, I'll be right back," before running to the cottage. When she returned at a walk, she was carrying a foil-covered pie plate. "Pumpkin, I made it myself."

I could not be prouder of her. "Oh man, that's fantastic, my favorite." I meant it and, not knowing how to appropriately touch her, I put a hand on her arm and said, "I didn't know you could cook."

"I'm just learning, and Marilyn's going to let me help with the dinner."

I figured that she would soon learn that I, the "Great and Wonderful Dex," was the chef in the family, but I didn't want to intrude at this point.

On the way home, I got a lesson in music on the radio, which I had not even turned on since buying the car. I was treated to Taylor Swift, Katy Perry, Adele, and others whose names were vaguely familiar. Still, I had known nothing of their music. The surprise was Emma's beautiful voice singing along with the radio. The next surprise would be when she found the newly tuned piano at home.

I had to thank Marilyn for that. As ordered by Sylvia, I had Googled for local piano tuners, and there was only one. I called and was told that there was no possibility that he could come before mid-December, *absolutely, positively, no way.* When I informed Marilyn of this problem, she took my phone, hit redial, and the man scheduled us for Friday morning, the week before the holiday. She burned me with the Cheshire Cat grin again and said, "Big Jim."

I parked at the back door, and Emma flew up the steps as I got her bag from the car. I heard sounds from the kitchen that I could only describe as "squealing." The girls were wrapped together when I got inside, bobbing up and down. The cat's body language showed that she was unsure of this commotion. Emma bent down and picked up the cat with teenage agility before it could bound away. She and Marilyn headed upstairs, arm in arm, while I followed like Sancho Panza, without the mule.

***

Tom and Mary Ellen arrived just before noon, bringing a lovely centerpiece. I purchased three bundles of wood at a convenience store. Tom also brought a couple of bottles of good wine. The initial introductions with Emma were a little awkward.

Still, she handled it well, looking lovely in a new sweater and slacks that Marilyn had bought. She was wearing a bright scarf around her neck, and last night had, apparently, brushed some raspberry-colored highlights into her dark brown hair. I learned later that the scarf covered a tattoo at the nape of her neck.

I placed their centerpiece on the dining table. The table was placed in front of the fireplace that had not seen flames in many years. I checked out the flue yesterday by burning a rolled-up newspaper, and it seemed alright.

Yesterday, I had bought a bottle of 12-year-old Macallan, also, a seltzer bottle and cartridges at Brookstone so we could enjoy Scotch and soda the old-fashioned way. Between that and the wine Tom and Mary Ellen brought, I felt awkward talking to Emma about the booze.

"Dex, I've been drinking since I was twelve and been drunk more times than I can count, but that was then. This is now. I'll pass on the Scotch, but may I have a glass of wine with the dinner?"

I was touched by her sincerity and that she asked my permission. "Of course, and remember, as hard as it is to imagine, I was once a teenager." We got a good laugh out of that, and I think we might have touched in some way, but I felt awkward doing so. I needed to talk with Marilyn about this.

***

Dinner was fantastic; it couldn't have been better. Emma and Marilyn were a cooking/serving /hosting team, and I carved the turkey. We all overate. While taking a break before the pie, Emma played some show tunes from old sheet music kept in the piano bench. She played pretty well, but we were stopped in our tracks when she sang. I saw little tears form at the corner of Marilyn's eyes.

Tom and I went out on the porch so he could smoke his annual cigar. His father did this; after his death, Tom decided to continue the tradition even though he was a non-smoker. He would light it, take a few puffs, wave it around to exaggerate his speech, and repeat the process when it went out. "Well, this is quite a family you've got now," he said, pointing with the cigar. "I'm glad you didn't see her the night she was arrested, Dex. It would have broken your heart."

"Thanks to you and Marty, we're giving her a chance. I think that's all she needed: people to trust her, love her, guide her, and just be a family to her. Dr. Englund thinks she's got the right stuff; we do, too. God, I hope we're right."

Emma's pie with coffee finished off the day. She was so proud of her accomplishment and complimentary reviews from everyone. Mary Ellen offered to help clean up, but Marilyn put her arm around Emma and said, "My assistant and I are all set." And then, pointing to me with a dessert fork, said, "I also have my slave." Emma was included in the laughter as I dropped my head and bowed to the queen.

After Tom and Mary Ellen left, I slumped in the recliner. Marilyn lay on the couch with an afghan and cat on top of her. Emma went upstairs to her room. She planned to be at Macy's by 5 a.m. before the doors opened for Black Friday shopping. She was taking my car, and I thought about her embarrassment when she offered to show me her driver's license, which bore the name Darlene. The girls at Meadowbrook were not allowed cell phones, so she would take mine. Marilyn asked her about money. She said she had enough, but that wasn't good enough for Marilyn, who pressed some bills into the large shoulder bag that Emma borrowed, so her hands were free for the shopping melee.

***

Emma woke just before the alarm with Black Friday anticipation. The red digits showed 4:15; it was pitch dark in the bedroom with no dawn yet in sight. Swinging her legs off the bed, she got up, eager to get dressed, get going, and get in line at Macy's before the doors opened at six o'clock. Dressing quickly in the new jeans and sweater Marilyn had bought her, she stuffed her hair under Marilyn's UConn stocking cap. Then put on a hoodie with a peace sign on the back.

She stepped into a pair of Uggs, slipped the bag shoulder strap over her head, and tiptoed down the back stairs to the kitchen. She was good to go with a quick glass of orange juice and the last piece of pie with another squirt of whipped cream. She slipped out the back door, drawing in her breath from the cold.

She parked far away from the store to avoid shopping cart damage. It started to rain in a cold drizzle, and the wind bit through her clothes. Her hands were tucked in the hoodie pocket, head down, hood up, shoulder bag lying across her front like a baseball catcher's protector.

There were about fifty people in line already, hunched and bunched against the cold. Some whispering, most just shifting from foot to foot, saying nothing. People kept coming and filling in behind her, the line rapidly extending around the corner of the building.

Someone cut in line behind her. "Hey, Darlene, I thought it was you."

She didn't have to turn to know the voice. "Fuck off, Terry, leave me alone."

"Fuck off? How 'bout we fuck on? Huh, it's been a while."

She turned her head and spit out, "I said, leave me alone!"

"Oh, so you don't need my car anymore. You're a big fucking deal now; no more muffin for miles, huh. Bitch!" He started to poke her back with a knuckle. "Darlene, Darlene, stroke my peen… hey, that rhymes… shit, I'm good."

She kept facing the front and hunched up more, trying to ignore this asshole.

"Darlene, Darlene, smoke my peen… hey, that's even better. So whatcha say, *D*, how 'bout it?"

She was gritting her teeth, trying to ignore him, breathing sharply. She swung an elbow back when he tried to get a hand under her hoodie but hit nothing. A security guard in a lime-colored slicker came over. "Hey, anything going on over here?"

Terry said, "We're good, officer, just joking around." Emma said nothing.

The guard backed away, putting three fingers in the air, saying to the crowd, "Three minutes, folks, three minutes. Okay, let's keep the line tight. Okay, two minutes… tighten up."

Emma felt Terry press into her and cringed, caught in the vice of this crowd. She thought she would faint, and her vision blurred when suddenly the doors opened, and the crest of the waiting crowd wave swept her into the store.

Terry was nowhere in sight. She got out of the crowd and settled behind the protection of a clothing display, trying to get herself back together. She was here to buy a Christmas gift for Marilyn and Dex: her family. Emma worked her way down the aisles as the first crush fanned out, and there was room to stop and look at the merchandise. She was unsure what the gift would be, but thought about something for music, maybe a CD player and some "older people" music.

She got as far as the kitchen appliances when she was tapped on her left shoulder. Surprised, she turned. "I told you to leave me alone!" She raised her voice and got right in his face.

Terry backed off, hands raised, suppliant. "Hey, no hard feelings. I'm leaving this shithole. Nothing but crap here. Just wanted to say goodbye… no hard feelings." He backed up, grinning.

She turned away, saying, "Asshole," through clenched teeth.

Time to get serious about the gift; stop poking around through the overwhelming displays. As she approached the electronics department, two people in blue blazers with an embroidered gold-colored crest on the pocket closed in on her.

The woman on her left side gripped her arm tightly and said, "Security; you're coming with us." The guy on her right took her bag.

"What are you doing?" Emma cried and tried to step back.

The security woman tightened her grip and snarled, "If you mess with me, I'll put you in cuffs and drag you. So you're coming with us."

"But, I…"

"Don't say another word. I don't want to hear it." The grip tightened, and Emma was swept toward the office, shocked and scared.

Emma was pushed inside when they got to the security office at the back of the store. The guy gave her back the bag, and the woman said, "Empty it on that table."

Emma held out her hands; I don't understand, what are…" She was trying hard not to cry. Finally, the woman said, "Empty it."

Mittens, tissues, car fob, Chapstick, *iPhone 6 with a small piece of display security cable attached.* Emma was bewildered, "I don't know where that…"

The Security woman grabbed her again and said, "Sit in that chair and keep your mouth shut," pointing to a metal folding chair in the corner.

Emma could hardly speak; her mouth was dry. "Ma'am, I…"

"Don't you, Ma'am me. I told you to shut up. You're under arrest for shoplifting. Glen, call the station." Emma began to cry.

Chapter 24

When I woke, I opened my eyes, and Marilyn was facing me in the bed, close, with open eyes and an adorable smile. She said, "Wasn't that a great time?" Not a question, a statement that I agreed with.

"It was wonderful for us and so much more for Emma... Jeez, Mar, I've missed so much in my life."

She put a hand on my shoulder, under the covers, saying, "You finally got the good things you deserve, Hon. It took a long time to get here, but it's worth it. I think she wants to call you Dad."

I closed my eyes and let that sink in, feeling pretty damn good about it.

***

I was making coffee; Marilyn was seated, moving a spoon aimlessly around the corners of a placemat when her phone rang. She fished it from her bathrobe pocket, checked the display, and mouthed, "Emma."

"Hi, shopper girl, how's the..." I watched the color drain from her face, and her free hand went to her hair, twisting a bunch in her fist. "Oh Jesus, oh God... honey, don't cry, I can't hear you... I can't hear you."

She held the phone out to me, her eyes imploring, unable to speak. I gripped the phone with a shaking hand, "What honey... what... tell me, what is it?"

All I heard was a mournful cry, "I didn't do it... I didn't do it." Repeated through waves of tears until a man's voice came on the line.

"Mr. Phillips, this is Detective Al Gray at Central Station. I'm sorry, but your daughter has been arrested for shoplifting at Macy's."

I couldn't speak, gripping the phone as if to squeeze the bad news out.

"Mr. Phillips, are you there? You need to come to the station before we can release her. Mr. Phillips?"

"Yes, we'll be right there. Is she alright? Can I talk with her again?"

"She's quite upset right now. I have a female officer with her. Probably best if you came right down."

We literally ran up the stairs. Marilyn stepped into sweats with her pajama bottoms still on and pulled a heavy sweater over her naked top. I slipped into yesterday's dress pants lying across the chair, threw on a sweatshirt, and laced up my shoes without socks. We ran down the stairs and grabbed yard coats off the hooks by the back door.

Marilyn pushed the garage door opener as soon as we were outside and said, "I'll drive. I'm faster than you."

We left the driveway at an alarming speed.

I don't know how we got that far without being stopped or crashed, but Marilyn pulled into the *POLICE CARS ONLY* slot at the front of the station in what could be considered record time. I pointed to the sign as she stopped. "Fuck 'em." Was her response as she ran up the sidewalk.

We burst into the lobby, looking like refugees, just as a man in a brown suit came through a door at the back wall. He stopped and held up both hands. "Hold on folks, she's okay, it's okay." He pumped his hands at us and added, "It's all settled. She didn't do anything. I just got the tapes."

We calmed down, but were still too stunned to start asking questions.

"C'mon down to my office; I want to show you some surveillance tapes we just downloaded." He held the door open, and we entered a long corridor.

Marilyn was the first to recover, saying, "I want to see Emma."

"She's okay, Mrs. Phillips, believe me. She's had the wind knocked out of her… figuratively. Let her rest a few minutes while I show you these tapes; it will explain everything."

We followed him down the hall to the door marked *Detectives* and entered a room with six cubicles. The one at the back left was occupied by a woman talking on the phone. Detective Gray motioned us to the nearest cubicle holding out the chair for Marilyn, then grabbed one from the next cubicle for me. He turned his monitor to face us, showing a grainy black and white picture of Macy's front entrance with a line of people waiting for the doors to open; the time stamp was 5:56 a.m. Scrolling the images, he stopped and pointed with a pen, saying, "Here's your daughter; watch this." He activated the screen, and it was clear that someone was bothering her from behind.

He scrolled further ahead. The store's interior came up; he stopped and said, "This guy," pointing with his pen. "That's the ass… sorry, the guy from outside who was bothering your daughter. Now, watch this," He went to freeze-frame and clicked one image at a time. "See, he looks around… has some tool in his hand. Picks up the iPhone in his left hand… comes across with his right… cuts the cord, and drops the phone in his pocket. That cable is alarmed, but nobody noticed with the store so busy."

I was fascinated by the scene, but my breath stopped when he zoomed in on the man's face. "I know that man." Marilyn looked at me, questioning as I added: "That's the kid who owned the VW." I got closer to the screen, suddenly realizing my fists were clenched.

"Okay, now watch this." The screen showed the man approaching store security, talking to him and pointing toward the back of the store. The guard turned and was talking on his hand-held radio. The man moved away and was lost in the crowd.

Marilyn leaned forward and excitedly said, "He's getting away." Pointing at the screen with a shaking finger.

Detective Gray said, "Now comes the fun part." He scrolled the screen toward the front of the store. "There's Emma," I said, gripping Marilyn's shoulder. We watched the thief come up behind Emma, tap her on the left shoulder, and drop the phone in her right-side bag when she turned.

Detective Gray froze the screen and said, "That's all we needed to see. Let's go find that little girl of yours."

We were speechless, but I was raging inside, and I'm sure Marilyn was, too. When we got to the interview room downstairs, Emma sat at a table, holding her hood down over her face. A Coke can was on the table in front of her. A female officer squatted beside her, saying something and slowly rubbing her shoulders.

I couldn't react, but Marilyn quickly went to Emma, holding her head to her breast and speaking quietly. The officer moved away from the table, nodded to Gray, and left the room. The detective and I were silent as Marilyn peeled back the hood, smoothed down the hair, and continued to speak softly. When Emma raised her head and looked at me, it was a face I never wanted to see again. She had cried her eyes out. What little makeup remaining from Thanksgiving had streaked down her face, and when she tried to speak, a little bubble of spit came out as she said, "I didn't do it." I'm sure I could have killed the guy with the VW at that moment.

The female officer returned with another Coke. I pulled up a chair for Marilyn, who still had her arm around Emma.

Detective Gray stood across the table and said, "Darlene, my sincere apology for what happened. I thank you for making the ID. I've got two officers out looking for him now. I talked to Marshall Simmons, the store manager, and he'll be calling you with an apology. You're a brave young woman who has been through a lot. Now go home with Mom and Dad and be safe."

He turned to me with an outstretched hand, saying, "I'm happy this turned out okay; your daughter seems like a great kid." I liked that; I didn't correct him. Then, he turned to Marilyn and Emma giving a kind of wave, saying, "Mrs. Phillips, Darlene, Officer Myers will show you out when you're ready."

Detective Gray was ahead of us as we went outside, and an officer was just about to ticket our car. Gray whistled and shook his head.

Marilyn and Emma got in the backseat where they could be close together. On the way home, I pulled into a Dunkin' to order an assorted dozen. "Get some jelly sticks," Marilyn called out the window.

"And a Boston Crème for me, Dad." I was suddenly ten feet tall.

When we got home, Emma sat upright, no longer clinging to Marilyn. The emotional resilience of our girl was incredible. When she got in the house, she picked up the cat, cuddled it, and whispered to it as though the cat was the one who'd been through hell. Then, she looked at us and said, "I'm going upstairs; I'm really beat… I'm going to lie down for a while."

"How about something to eat?" Marilyn asked. "Are you hungry.?"

"I'm good; the donut filled me up. I just need a little rest." She came to Marilyn, still carrying the cat, and said, "Thanks, Mom," and kissed her cheek.

I had just come in the back door to see that. She came to me, hesitated for a moment, then said, "Thanks, Dad, for everything." She reached out and squeezed my arm, and the cat put a soft paw on her cheek.

Shortly after Emma went upstairs, Marilyn said, "I'm going upstairs checking on her." When she left, I went to the cupboard and got out the remains of the Macallan. Marilyn returned to the kitchen and sat at the table across from me. I raised the glass in a question, she nodded, and I got up for another glass.

As I was pouring, she said, "She's sleeping now, she and the cat. But you know what she said?" Then, without waiting for my reply, she continued, "She feels sorry for that guy, Terry. Can you believe it? I'd like to rip his nuts off. She said he's had a hard life, and it will not get any better. He's got a learning disability and quit school when he was sixteen and only got to the tenth grade. So he's not going anywhere, Dex; it's a shame, a terrible shame."

As she talked, I felt my hands closing into fists when his name was spoken. But I had to admit, I felt sorry for him, too. None of these kids were born evil. We, the supposed grown-ups and start the problems that bury these kids for the rest of their lives. I relaxed my hands and felt even more determined that Emma would not suffer a similar fate.

Chapter 25

Saturday morning, I woke after a restless sleep. Emma would be going back to Meadowbrook tomorrow. I slipped out of bed, trying not to wake Marilyn. I looked out the window and decided the weather was too blustery to shoot baskets this early in the morning.

I was surprised to see the light in my office and found Emma sitting in the desk chair with Marilyn's laptop in her lap. She was concentrating on the screen, lightly tapping her teeth with the blunt end of a pen… *tic… tic… tic.* I called from the doorway, "Hey, sweet girl, what are you up to?"

As I approached, she tilted her head back, smiling, and said with a grin, "About five-foot-five."

"Wise guy," I tousled her hair.

"I must write an essay for school about an event during the holiday. So I'm writing about yesterday."

I blew out some air, sat in the chair next to the desk, and said, "Are you sure you want to go through that again?"

She looked right at me, "Mrs. Patterson said we could fictionalize it if we wanted, and I thought you could help me with that."

"Let's see what you've got so far."

She handed me the laptop, and I tilted the screen to read:

THE BLACKEST FRIDAY

By Emma Phillips

I was startled by her name, but said nothing except, "Catchy title," and then read the text.

It was cold and raining a little. The shadows in the early morning darkness were penetrated in places by tall lights in the parking lot.

I was standing in line with a lot of other people, waiting for the store to open at six o'clock to rush in for the holiday bargains.

A guy cut in line behind me and started to pester me. I told him several times to quit it! Finally, I called to the security guy in the lime green raincoat with reflective strips on the arms. He came over and told the guy to stop bothering me, and then the doors opened, and I was swept into the store like a wave at the beach.

While I was shopping, the guy that was bothering me came up and tapped me on the shoulder. When I turned that way, he dropped something into my open shoulder bag on my right side. I didn't know it.

What he dropped in was an iPhone he had just stolen, but I didn't know. I told him to get lost. But he went to security and told them he saw me shoplifting and I had something in my bag.

They came up and arrested me and were very rude, and I tried to tell them I didn't do anything, and they took me to their office.

They made me empty my bag, and there it was. I was scared, and they called the downtown cops. Who came and put me in a cruiser. I was taken to the station and put in a room.

The room had a table and two chairs. They told me to sit in one, and a-woman cop stood there watching over me. She didn't say anything.

And then, this detective came in and questioned me. I kept telling them I didn't do it. I was scared and began to cry. He called my parents.

When they came to the station, they were ripping mad, not at me. But the detective had got surveillance tapes from the store that showed what had happened and that I was innocent. The woman cop got me a Coke and was very friendly. My mother hugged me, and my dad put an arm around my shoulders as we went out to the car. On the way home, we got donuts at Dunkin'.

It was the blackest Friday of my life, except for the part about my parents.

E.P.

"Wow! That's good; I'll be right back; I need a bathroom." I barely got out of the room before the tears started stinging, and by the time I got to the kitchen, I couldn't speak. Marilyn had just come down the back stairs to the kitchen and looked at me, startled.

I cross-waved my hands in an *it's okay, but I can't talk now* gesture and went outside. I walked down the driveway, in my bathrobe, toward the street so Emma couldn't see me from the office window. The emotional blitz was overwhelming. I stayed there a few minutes, then went in and washed my eyes at the kitchen sink. Apparently, Marilyn had taken a coffee back upstairs.

Emma had made copies in the office, signed them, and handed one to me. She heard Marilyn coming down the stairs and turned quickly to greet her. "Hi, Mom," She called brightly and moved to give her the paper. No gift ever meant so much.

***

Later in the morning, I put the rented party equipment on the front porch to make it easier for them to pick up when my phone lit up with a number I didn't recognize.

"Good morning, Mr. Phillips; this is Marshall Simmons, the store manager at Macy's. I'm just calling to apologize to your daughter for the Friday incident."

I wasn't sure how to respond, so I tried not to show my anger. "Just a minute."

I went inside where the girls were preparing to bake a cake. "Emma, The Macy's manager is calling; he wants to apologize." Then saying loudly enough so Simmons could hear, "Do you want to speak to him, or should I just tell him no?"

She surprised me when she took the phone, turned away, and coldly spoke, "Yes… yes… no, keep it! I'll never go to your store again." Then, she moved into the living room and continued talking on the phone. Finally, she returned to the kitchen and handed me the phone saying, "That creep wanted to give me a fifty-dollar gift certificate."

Mom and Dad were beaming. Marilyn said, "I'm surprised you didn't call him a nasty name."

"I did. You just didn't hear it." We all broke into laughter and high fives, then a group hug — God, what a family.

***

This would be our last night together until the Christmas break. I suggested we go to a restaurant for dinner, but Emma said she would rather stay home and pig out on a big bucket of extra-crispy KFC. So after greasing up our guts with that, we sat in the living room with Emma playing show tunes from the old book, and we all sang along. She played pretty well for the limited lessons she had received at Meadowbrook, but her potential was evident. She and Marilyn harmonized on some of the songs from *Guys and Dolls,* which was a favorite of mine.

Marilyn made popcorn that we picked at while watching SNL before wrapping up for the night. Nothing was said about Emma's return to school the next day, but it was certainly on my mind.

They went upstairs together; Mar wanted to sit with her for a while and girl talk. So I went into my office and reread *The Blackest Friday*. I thought about how little we know about what this girl has been through all these years. I was swiveling slowly back and forth in the chair when Marilyn came in and said, "I saw her tattoo."

"What, how did… ?"

"She put her hair up, and I could see it at the nape of her neck. So I asked her if it had hurt, and she said a little, then told me she was probably drunk."

I started to speak. But Marilyn continued with, "It just makes me shiver when I think about her out there with no family, no place, nothing but herself against a shitty world."

I put a hand up. Marilyn grasped it tightly in both of hers as if to anchor herself against a storm. "What kind of tattoo is it… I mean, like the design?"

She released my hand and sat in the chair by the desk, clasping her hands between her knees. "She said it's a *compass rose*. I guess there's a lot of history to it. Sailors had it done years ago as a good luck charm to get them home safely. So now she has a home, Dex, she's safe. Marilyn moved her hands to her face and hunched over a little. I rolled my chair around and put my hands on her knees. We sat like that for several minutes without saying a word.

***

Sunday morning was relaxed; I got the paper, and we lay around drinking coffee, dunking the stale donuts from Friday, and ended up watching *Meet the Press.* Emma was surprised at the political jousting and interested in the program. Her world was beginning to expand in many ways. She had to be back at Meadowbrook by three, and told me there were rumors that girls arriving late were never seen again. She said that in good humor, and we were all feeling good. There didn't seem to be any foreboding about her return, and we discussed the coming Christmas holiday and when we would be together again. Something for which I had already made plans.

***

When we returned to her cottage, one girl was entering the cottage with her mother.

Emma said, "C'mon, Mom, mothers are allowed inside. Not so much for fathers, sorry, Dad," she said, gripping my arm and kissing my cheek before bouncing up the walk hand in hand with Marilyn.

I spotted Sylvia coming out of the next cottage and called her, raising a hand in a 'got a minute gesture. She waved back and started walking toward me.

"How was your holiday?" She said, extending a hand, looking relieved that it was over.

"We had no idea what having a teenage girl in the house would be like. It was an incredible adventure, but I'm sure Emma will give you all the details. In fact, she wrote her assignment about a pretty serious situation."

"Oh?"

"Yes, she had a little problem, but handled it well and came out of it stronger than ever. But I want to ask you about the Christmas holiday. According to your schedule, the girls are dismissed on the twenty-third. Although I'd like to pick up Emma the day before, I have some plans.

"Dex, you know the rules…."

"I was thinking, if I came here a day early, that would give me time to write a donation check to the school."

She laughed, punched me lightly in the arm, and said, "Now you're talking my language."

"Thanks, see you then… please don't say anything about any plans to my girls. It's a Christmas surprise."

"Got it, Dex, you take care." She turned and headed to the next cottage. For some reason, I had ceased to be offended by "take care."

Marilyn came out smiling, with no sign of tears. "How'd it go?" I asked when she got in the car.

"It's great, Dex; the place has a nice vibe. Unfortunately, I saw her room but didn't get to meet her roommate, who's not back yet from New Jersey. But I did get to meet Mrs. Patterson, and I like her a lot."

"You're not crying, Mar."

"What's to cry about. I'm happy as a pig in shit. Let's go to that tavern and get a drink." She said, smiling, as she buckled in.

Chapter 26

It had been an exhausting weekend. In fact, more than four days were filled with all the drama of our personal reality show. I slipped out of bed Monday morning, trying not to wake Marilyn, and stood there looking at her. She was turned away from me, her hair splayed across the pillow, covers pulled up, and her hands tucked under her chin as if praying. I could see a few gray hairs she missed in her pre-holiday touch-up. Something she did not talk about. Her breathing was slow and soft. I knew she'd be warm to the touch. I wanted to kiss her, but that would wake her, and I had secret plans for this morning.

Last night, I casually placed clothes on a chair while she was reading a romance novel in bed. So, I gathered them up and dressed in my office, where I had left my shoes. I was desperate for coffee but didn't want to chance it here, and I quietly slipped out the back door.

When I pushed the opener remote, the garage door rose with enough noise to wake the dead. I went to the garage and entered the car with the damn key alert sounding like the bells of St. Paul's Cathedral. I used the "ostrich defense" against Marilyn at times like these. If I can't see her, she can't see me. I made it out of the driveway without being stopped.

First, I needed coffee at Dunkin'. So I joined the drive-up line, ordered, and headed to Destinations Travel.

Natalie, the woman who booked my first Arizona trip, was on the phone when I arrived, and Amy offered to help at her desk. I thanked her and said I would wait.

Natalie finished her call and rose, hand extended, "Mr. Phillips, happy to see you again. How can I help you?"

I explained my need for three tickets to Phoenix and gave her the dates. She attacked her keyboard with a speed I didn't think was humanly possible and booked us an entire outside row; *41 A, B, and C.*

I sat in the parking lot for a few minutes, reveling in my plan. My stomach was uneasy, and I blamed that on the coffee and the anxiety. However, I finally admitted that I hadn't felt well for the past two weeks, blaming that on the recent stresses. I headed for a CVS and some Nexium, tucking the surprise tickets in the console.

***

I was hoping to make it home before Marilyn woke, but soon knew it was a fool's errand. She was sitting at the kitchen table with the coffee cup and the remains of some toast. "Where have you been?"

"Tom's."

"Tom Brandt doesn't get out of bed until ten."

"Not always." I thought I could slip by and put the tickets in my desk drawer.

"Hold it!"

"What?"

She gave me her mongoose stare that fixed me in place. "Is this another one of your surprises?"

"Maybe." I waved an arm as if to dismiss any thought of subterfuge. The envelope started slipping from beneath my jacket. She put her hand out, not saying anything. I put it in her hand and went upstairs to change.

I had one leg in my jeans when I heard them pounding up the stairs. Little steps from the cat, then Marilyn. She burst into the room like a Midwest tornado, grabbed a pillow off the unmade bed, and started beating me with it. I was laughing so hard; she had the advantage, pushed me onto the bed and started tickling my ribs. I couldn't stop laughing until she stopped tickling, kissed my face, and got off the bed to remove her pajamas, commanding, "Get your clothes off!"

***

Later in the day, Marilyn called her sisters with the news. I could only hear one side of the conversation, but it was easy to figure out the excitement from the ranch. Marilyn gave Emily all of Emma's sizes so she could have a Southwest wardrobe waiting. That evening, we went to Zapata's Mexican Cantina to start conditioning our stomachs, and then on to Kohl's to get some traveling clothes for Emma. I marveled at the joy this simple act brought to Marilyn. It also allowed me to continue a tradition started by my father. So I slipped a C-note into the bell ringer's Salvation Army kettle.

***

I wasn't sure Mar could get through the next few weeks without exploding from sheer happiness. She talked expectantly about *Emma in Arizona.* Emma in the pool, going shopping, sightseeing, the San Carlos reservation. Marilyn had worked out a staggering itinerary for mother and daughter. I was delighted for them, but planned to spend most of my time sucking up margaritas by the pool.

Into every life, a little rain must fall. And for Marilyn, it was a cloudburst. She suddenly remembered the cat who hadn't traveled well on the previous flight, and she was reluctant to put her through that again. So she Googled local catteries, there were three, but instead of just phoning an inquiry, we had to inspect them first.

We visited all three, where she asked for qualifications and references. She questioned the care, the feeding, the companionship, and the playtime. She stated veiled threats about what would happen if she were to return home and find the cat unhealthy and unhappy. She finally decided on Kitty Kastle, and I had difficulty keeping a straight face as she left the final instructions.

***

I stopped at the office to give Sylvia a donation and check my balance from my original 10K. She greeted me warmly and offered me a glass of wine.

We stood by the fireplace, and she told me of the counseling session she had with Emma, reviewing *The Blackest Friday* essay. "She did a good job on the assignment, Dex, but it was evident there was much more to read between the lines. I think they scared the crap out of her, and I admire her courage." She took a sip of wine. "And I admire the way you and Marilyn supported her. Did you condemn her when you first got the news?"

I thought for a minute. "No, I honestly don't think we ever felt that way. In fact, I thought Mar was quite combative in her defense of Emma. For example, did Emma tell you about the store manager calling?"

"She did."

"That was priceless."

"What do you think of her new name — Emma Phillips?"

"We like it, and she's calling us Mom and Dad. We like that."

"You understand she may legally change her name to Phillips, but you're under no obligation to adopt or anything like that."

"Sylvia, we love her as she is or how she wants to be. She's part of our family. I mean, what the hell? Mar and I aren't married, but we're as close as possible. And Emma is part of that closeness.

"Nice to hear that, Dex." She clinked my glass and said, "Let's drink to that and a Merry Christmas to your family.

***

Parked outside her cottage with two other cars containing, I assumed, fathers, I felt like I was part of a fraternal organization. Emma came out the door, waved, hugged the mother and daughter who had exited with her, and came running to the car with excitement I could feel through the glass.

"Hi, Dad," Emma kneeled across the seat, kissed my cheek, settled and buckled, and then found some rock station to groove on as we headed home. I kept looking at her, thinking of her anticipation for the long holiday recess and how she would react to the trip. Finally, Mar and I decided to keep it a surprise, and she would know nothing until we got to the airport.

At home, after the mother/daughter hugs and kisses, she said, "Where's the cat?"

I looked at Marilyn, who could not tell a lie, and she said, “Visiting.”

“What, who?” Emma was squinty-eyed.

I joined the conversation, “We thought she needed some socialization.”

Emma stepped back, cocked her head, and said, “You guys are bullshitting me.” Then, in horror, “Oh my God, she died!”

Marilyn stepped in quickly and bravely put the onus on me. “She’s part of your father’s plan.”

“What plan?” She turned her teenage wrath on me.

“I… um… can't tell you.”

She caught right on that this had something to do with Christmas. “Okay, with you guys, I can play that game, too.” She punched me on the arm and went upstairs.

***

The jig was up as soon as we took the airport exit. The next big surprise was the check-in for Phoenix. “Oh, my God… oh, my God… oh, my God.” She hugged us and said, “I’ve never been on a plane.”

I got up twice from the boarding area to go to the men’s room. The second time I took the purple pill; I had forgotten in all the rush this morning.

Chapter 27

After take-off, during which she had her eyes closed and hand held tightly with Marilyn's, Emma was glued to the window, marveling at the clouds and patchwork of the earth below. As we crossed the mountains and the desert around Phoenix, she became apprehensive about the landing and latched onto Marilyn's hand again. When Sky Harbor International came into view, Emma was too excited to be scared. She kept her eyes open, bouncing Marilyn's hand up and down with excitement.

While I gathered our bags, Mar phoned her sister, who came from the parking lot to pick us up at the terminal. It was so crowded at the curb that Linda stayed behind the wheel.

Emily jumped out to greet us, taking Emma by the arms, holding her out for inspection, then hugged her and said, "You beautiful girl, welcome to our family." I saw little tears come to the corner of Marilyn's eyes that she wiped away before hugging her sister.

"Dammit, Dex, it's good to see you again; Brian's been asking for his 'burrito buddy." Emily kissed my cheek. We climbed into the SUV and got a quick greeting from Linda as a terminal cop was approaching, blowing his whistle and waving us to get out of there.

On the way back to the ranch, I sat there in silence. There was no chance to get a word in among those three females.

I had the shotgun seat next to Linda. The three girls were behind me, talking excitedly. I could see Emma in the mirror, and she seemed to be caught in sensory overload as she swiveled her head left and right, taking in the sights that rushed by as we headed north of Phoenix.

When we came to the ranch drive entrance, I unclicked my seatbelt and turned to watch her expression. Jaw-dropping was the only way to describe it. She was open-mouthed, speechless. When we got out of the car, Emily said, "Wait 'till you see it at night. We had a crew come in and string the whole damn place with Christmas lights; it's spectacular."

Marilyn took Emma's arm and led her into the house. "C'mon girl, we've got stuff to do."

I grabbed the bags, Emily left for a business appointment, and Linda headed for the kitchen to make margaritas and snacks.

"Mom, I can't believe this… I honestly can't believe this." Emma's head was going in circles.

"It's only the beginning, hon'. You ain't seen nothin' yet." Marilyn led her down the wide corridor to the patio and pool. They stopped briefly as Emma put a hand to her mouth and made squeaky little noises. In the guest suite, several clothing outfits were laid out on the bed, all good choices by Emily for a teenage girl, including a swimsuit. Emma began to cry. This girl, who had endured so much difficulty, was overwhelmed by this display.

She turned to Marilyn and buried her face in her breast, sobbing and shaking, seeming weak in the knees. Mar sat her down on the bed, holding her close, whispering and smoothing her hair. Emma worked her way down to sobs and hiccups and said, "Mom, Dad, Aunt Linda, Aunt Emily. I thank you from the bottom of my heart… I really do." She wiped her eyes and nose on her sleeve and said, "Can I put on the swimsuit?"

"Whatever you want, hon', there's no schedule. We're here on vacation. I want to warn you, though…" Emma looked at her, and Marilyn said, "Dad likes to do cannonballs in the pool."

They laughed at that, and Emma said, "That could be a problem."

"Why is that?"

"I don't know how to swim."

"Oh, sweetheart," Mar hugged Emma again, "I'll teach you."

Then, looking more closely at the swimsuit, Marilyn said, "Wait a minute… there's not much to that thing."

"Oh, Mom."

"Yeah, well, I'm going to say something to Emily about her selection. I'll see you at the pool. You put a shirt on over that."

***

While the girls were next door, I had changed into my swimsuit and was already poolside, adjusting the sunshade over the chaise. I was disappointed the tan I had achieved here two months ago had been forfeited back in Connecticut.

Linda came out with the drinks cart and several platters of super-looking snacks. "So, glad to see you guys back here and to meet Emma; she's perfect. We're such a small family, so to be graced by someone like her is like having a new life."

I answered for both of us, "That's exactly what we're trying to give her, Lin, a new life. The old one was pretty tough."

"You know, Dex, you brought Marilyn back to life, and we're so damn grateful. And now you've opened your hearts to this young lady. We're grateful… that's what we are, grateful." I never expected tears from Linda. Instead, she took one of the cocktail napkins, wiped her eyes, bent down, kissed my cheek, said, "grateful" again, and returned to the kitchen. I poured my first margarita into a salt-rimmed stem glass, bit a slice of lime, and poured the second as my ladies came out to the pool.

Marilyn had a towel over her suit. Emma did not. I looked at Mar, who rolled her eyes and said, "Emily's choice; I'll talk with her." So, we were getting into parenting.

In Arizona, it was legal for people under twenty-one to have a drink if they were at home with their parents. I was pouring for Linda and Marilyn. I looked at Emma at Mar's side and she nodded, holding up one finger. So much for proper parenting. We raised our glasses and said, "To the good times, Merry Christmas."

On Christmas Eve morning, Brian drove up, followed by a red convertible containing his daughter, a freshman at Arizona State, and her roommate, a girl from Oregon. They were here to take Emma on a local tour. In addition, Brian was here to take me to the latest burrito challenge.

After the introductions, we watched three happy girls laughing their way to a good time. Then, as I got in his truck, Brian said, in Irish fashion, "Good on ya, Dex, and to Marilyn. Your Emma is a beautiful girl."

Responding with my phony Irish accent, I said, "Tanks, Bri, I canna tell ya what she means t' us." Then with a bit of sadness, I added, "It also shows me how much I've lost over all these years," Brian reached over and put his hand on my shoulder for a moment as we headed out the drive.

***

I could only describe the burritos as "nuclear." Two Dos Equis later, I thought I might survive.

"Damn good burritos, hey, Dex?"

"Shit yeah, really good," I managed to say without gasping like a rookie.

Heading back to the ranch, I was suddenly thrust forward against the seat restraint by a sharp pain pushing through my guts. I cried out and then couldn't breathe.

"Dex… Dex… what's wrong… hold on." Brian brought the truck to a stop at the side of the desert just beyond the breakdown lane. I managed to get out of the seatbelt and open the door, leaning heavily against it as I fell out of the truck.

"Jesus, Dex…" Brian ran around the truck, putting an arm around me and keeping me on my feet. Suddenly, the pain was gone. "Holy shit… that was bad, Brian. A fucking burrito attack, I guess. That sonofabitch is not giving up easily." I tried to laugh but started choking on a bit of bile and bent over to spit that out.

"Good Jesus, Dex, you scared the shit out of me. Are you okay?"

"Good as gold in them thar hills," I said, pointing to the distant mountains, trying to humor my way out of whatever happened. "Yeah, I'm okay now."

When we were driving again, he said, "Jesus, good buddy, you scared the shit out of me." But of course, I didn't say I was beginning to get a little worried myself.

***

On our return, we stopped at two building sites where Brian proudly showed me their new designs. Gorgeous homes built with quality construction. "Big Jim's legacy," he said, sweeping a hand at the houses.

When we returned to the ranch, he said, "Dex, you take care. You've got family now." *Ain't that the truth.*

Marilyn had strung a nylon rope with spaced blue and white floats across the pool's shallow end. She was bent over, demonstrating proper breathing techniques to Emma. Biting a breath, releasing it on the downstroke, smooth, easy. "Now, you try it."

Emma pushed off the poolside, swam halfway across before losing the rhythm, and stood up sputtering. I cheered and clapped and felt so proud. Emma laughed and tried to splash me.

I still felt a little ragged from my stomach episode. Although I would like to go in the pool, I decided to sit and let things settle. Lying back on the chaise, eyes closed, I marveled at our good fortune. The girls were done with the swim lesson and headed to their rooms to shower and change.

"Emma, let me show you this," Marilyn took her in to see our tropical rainforest bathroom.

"Oh, my God." She shook her head in amazement. "Do you and Dad shower in here together?" She said, pointing to the glass enclosure.

Marilyn didn't respond.

"I bet you do," Emma added with a giggle.

"That's none of your business, young lady. Now can I have some privacy?"

Emma headed to the door, turned, and said again, "Bet you do." It was no longer a question in her mind.

***

It was Christmas Eve, and Emily said Jeff was coming — and hinted something special might happen.

Linda told Marilyn that she'd begun to see Roger again, but that he was spending the holiday with his son's family and the grandchildren.

"How's it going with you and Roger?" Marilyn asked as they were in the kitchen working on dinner.

"Pretty good. I think I'll let him into my heart," Linda said thoughtfully.

"Oh, for Christ's sake, Lin, you've got to do better than that."

"Maybe."

***

When it was dark enough, we went out front, and Linda turned on the decorative lights. It was spectacular. The Fitzgerald construction crew had run colored lights on every roof edge and fixed a decorated tree to the chimney that rose out of the great room. Back inside, there was Christmas music playing from speakers in every room. The courtyard surrounding the pool was bathed in colored lighting that changed hues every thirty seconds. It was beautiful, but the crew had gone a little over the top to impress the boss.

Emma stayed with the women, helping get things ready for the meal. Jeff and I remained outside with drinks in our hands, talking about stuff. I liked Jeff and was interested in his work with the BLM. But I said, "I don't know how you do it; there's got to be a lot of heartaches."

"There is, Dex, but the feeling is indescribable for every good outcome when we save a horse, and it goes on to a good home and good life. We constantly get letters, emails, and Facebook posts showing happy outcomes." When he said that, I thought of Emma. He continued, "The wild horses are America; it's our obligation to save them." I asked him how I could contribute.

***

After the meal, Jeff stood up and raised his wine glass. "Okay, folks, time for the big announcement." He paused while we all stared in attention. "I'm pleased to announce..." He took a sip of wine, raised the glass and repeated, "I'm pleased to announce that... my alma mater, Arizona State, is ranked third in this year's NCAA basketball..." Emily hit him with her napkin. We all started laughing, and then he shouted, "Emily and I are getting married," pumping his arm in the air amid our cheers and congratulations.

It was a magic moment, and I squeezed Marilyn's hand under the table.

Linda brought out two bottles of champagne, and we all toasted the future bride and groom. Emma raised her glass and said, "Your happiness is my happiness. I thank you all so much." We cheered her, and she held a napkin to her face as Marilyn gently rubbed her shoulders.

***

The magic was over. Emily said goodbye, hugging and kissing her sisters and Emma. Then she and Jeff left, but not before she gripped my arm and said, "You're the best, Dex." I accepted that gratefully and turned away, wiping my eyes on my sleeve.

When we got to the airport in the morning, it was much less crowded than when we arrived, and Linda could get out of the car for a final round of goodbye hugs.

***

Nine hours later, my only thought was, "It's so fucking cold," as I stamped my feet and fumbled the car door fob. I picked up Mar and Emma at the terminal, handing them the winter coats we had left in the car. Marilyn sat in front with me, all tightened up, waiting for the heater to throw out some warmth. Emma was lying across the back seat. I think she was asleep before we got out of the access road.

Chapter 28

By the time we got home, and into the house, I thought I'd fall over from exhaustion. Mar helped a sleepy Emma up the stairs while I brought the bags inside and put the car away. It felt like it could snow tonight.

I locked up and raised the thermostat two degrees for a little more heat, turned out the lights, and went upstairs to find Marilyn hunkered under the covers, snoring lightly. Emma's door was closed, and there was no sign of light underneath.

I sat in a chair for a while, hearing the hot water circulate through the baseboard pipes and listening to my heart. Everything seemed okay. I figured the incident with the burrito attack was an aberration brought on by an errant jalapeno. Since then, I'd felt pretty good. When I returned, I decided to call Dick Doc and had to fight with myself not to cancel that idea. I'd call in the morning.

***

I was surprised that Marilyn was not in bed when I awoke. It was now a quarter past eight. I hoped nothing was wrong.

I went downstairs to find her fully clothed, well into her second cup of coffee, and looking very happy. This was weird.

"What's going on, Mar? You're up early."

"I'm going to pick up the cat."

"They don't open until ten."

"I know. I just want to be ready."

Sometimes her logic confused me. I could only respond by saying, "I think Emma had a good time."

"Are you kidding? She had a *great* time. We talked for quite a while on the plane while you were sleeping, and she asked me about something else."

"What's that?" I asked as I got up for a paper towel to mop up the coffee I had just spilled.

"She'd like to go to college this next trimester at Marlborough Community College. It starts on January 19. What do you think?"

"Why not? She's smart enough, she's got her GED, and it sounds like she's got the desire. Has she any idea of where this is going?"

"She'd like to get a teaching certificate or be a writer *like you.*"

Those last words stung a little, but I brushed it off, determined to return to my book soon. "Has she been thinking about this for a while.?"

"A little while, I guess, but being with Brian's daughter and her roommate opened her eyes. She can do it, Dex; I know she can. She only wants to take two courses because she wants to do well, and, also, she wants to work part-time."

"Wow! The times they are a-changin." What does she plan to do… for work?"

"I asked her, and she said she'd like to get into an office, learn some skills, and spend more time on a computer. She definitely doesn't want to sling burgers or pour coffee. She said, *that's for kids*. She's growing up fast."

"She's not planning on leaving, is she?" I asked with alarm.

"No, of course not; she's just growing up."

"I'll call Tom; he'll know of something." Marilyn was putting her coat on. I said, "Where are you going? They don't open for another forty minutes."

"Maybe there's a queue."

I waited a few minutes after she cleared the driveway. Marilyn had a habit of doubling back to get some items she forgot in her usual haste. Once it was all clear, I would call Dick Doc.

"Lane residence, good morning."

"Hi, Suzy, it's Dex. Is the grumpy old bastard awake yet?"

"Hey, Dex, good to hear from you. We stopped by the other day, and your house was dark. Were you away for the holiday?"

"Yeah, we went to Arizona, Marilyn's family home, a ranch. We took our daughter."

"Yeah, Dicky told me about her. We'd love to meet her. I'll call Marilyn about lunch or something… hold on, I hear him coming in. He's been out jogging."

Dick Lane came on the phone, still breathing a little fast. "Hey, Dex."

"Dicky, my man, I'll buy you a cheap sandwich at the alleys if you're available."

"A beer, too?"

"Maybe."

"I'll see you at noon."

***

Instead of sitting at the bar as usual, I picked out a quiet booth. I think he knew right away I had something important to say after we finished the sandwiches. So, I signaled the bar for two more beers and said, "I'm looking for medical advice."

"So, why don't you go to a doctor?"

"I probably will; I just wanted to ask your opinion first." Dick's face began to cloud up, and he leaned closer across the table as if to examine me.

I told him as much as I could recall about my symptoms, especially the Arizona burrito attack.

He sat back, staring at me, biting his lower lip. "I'm an eye guy, Dex. But frankly, I don't like the sound of this."

"So, scare me some more."

"Someone has to, you stupid shit. Did you think you'd find a cure in the drugstore? You need to get to an internist, or better yet, an oncologist."

I thought he might say that, but it slammed me anyway. I sat there for a minute, pursing my lips in and out, then said, "I expected you might say that. Do you have any names?"

"There's a woman in the office suite next to my daughter's. You know where that is, my old office." He took a small pad and pen as though he were still dispensing scrip and wrote *Dr. Tracey Kim.* "My daughter is very impressed with her. She's the only name I can think of. All my old buddies are retired or worse." He pushed the note across the table. And put his hand on top of mine when I reached for it. He looked straight at me and said, "Do it today! I'll call my daughter and tell her to contact Doctor Kim. I'll let you know what happens."

"Another one?" I said, raising my empty bottle.

"Why not."

***

After the call, I sat in the car, thinking of all the people with problems more significant than mine. The ones who had to wait days or weeks for an appointment. I was scheduled for 10:30 the next day. Now my next problem was Marilyn. I solved that by calling Dicky to thank him and having him call me early tomorrow, needing help at his house with something so I could get out of the house unquestioned. I thought I was back in junior high.

***

When I got home, my girls were gone. *SHOPPING* was all the note said. This could mean anything from a pair of socks to a new car in Marilyn's mind. But I thought it had something to do with college clothes.

I called Tom and explained about Emma's quest for a part-time job. As expected, he knew someone. He always did. For a guy who quit working ten years ago, he still had his finger on the pulse. "I'll make some calls and get back to you, Dex. How was Arizona?" I gave him all the good stuff, not saying anything about burritos or my lunch with Dicky.

The cat appeared, stretching, working its claws in and out, recovering from her sleep job in some secluded place. I picked her up and held her to my ear, listening to that little motor hum, trying not to feel sorry for myself. I needed to have the strength of Charlie Osbourne. As I stroked her fur, I noticed a new seasonal-themed breakaway collar. Little red roses and what appeared to be holly leaves embossed on a field of light blue. The roses made me think of Emma's compass rose tattoo. I needed a distraction, and the book would give me that.

I stopped writing my narratives on paper. Finally, feeling comfortable with the Word program on the computer. I entered them on the keyboard, storing these narratives in a *My Life Stories* file. I called this one:

THE TATTOO

On my first three-day pass from Fort Dix, I went into New York City with one of my buddies to get tattoos. There was a hole-in-the-wall shop operated by a guy named Ace Benedict. All the guys in my unit swore by his artful skill.

Although we felt we were tough enough to withstand the needles, we thought it was best to get a little liquid courage and stopped in a nearby bar for a shot and a beer. But, of course, Ace wouldn't do a tattoo if a person was too drunk. Some sort of tattoo artist moral code, or something legal, I didn't know.

He opened at 4 p.m. There wasn't much morning tattoo business, but there was a line in front of the store waiting for him to open.

We recognized one of the guys from our unit and asked some questions. He peeled back the short sleeve on his right arm and showed us something that looked like a solid black cow trailing ribbons of brownish cow shit. "Beautiful, ain't it," he said with a thick southern accent, not as a question for us to answer. "The fucking thing is supposed to be a panther with yellow eyes and claws digging into my fucking muscle. Shit! The guy that did this should have his balls tattooed. I hope Ace can fix this for me."

The only girl in the line turned and showed us her wrist tattoo. A winding wreath of red and green spelling "Bobby."

I showed my attention, "Nice work."

"Hell yeah, but the guy I'm marrying next week is, "Ron."

Maybe we should have had another round at the bar because we began to see a problem here. We would have booked it if Ace hadn't arrived when he did.

He was a little guy, maybe mid-fifties, kind of swarthy looking, but otherwise clean. His glasses had thick lenses, and I worried about that, but everybody swore by his work. He carried a small satchel, like a kid's play doctor bag. I don't know if it contained some tattoo tools, his lunch, or a gun.

When we filed into the small shop, my buddy and I went to the display wall on the right to check out the flash. Each design had a number.

Ace was talking to our buddy with the cow tattoo. "There's not much I can do with this piece of crap except go bigger and all black. It'll go mostly around your arm." I tried not to appear to be listening, but every word was recorded in doubt. Nevertheless, Ace was highly recommended, and I was determined.

Before he started on the girl, I said, "Hey, Ace, can I see the flash for 23 and 138?" So, Ace went to some slotted drawers in a narrow cabinet and took out the transfer patterns so I could lay them on my arm and see how they fit.

"And what can I do for you, young lady?" I could hear Ace laying on the charm. When she showed him the problem, he studied it a minute, opened a cabinet drawer, took out a transfer, and laid it over her wrist. She said, "Oh, Jesus, that's horrible." And began to cry.

I've got to hand it to Ace. He was sympathetic to the girl and offered several more suggestions. Still, she left there intending to have it surgically removed.

I asked for numbers 65, 67, and 191.

The next guy in line wanted nothing to do with getting a tattoo fixed. He wanted it gone. I listened to Ace explain the procedure available in those days and the remaining scarring. Finally, the guy left, all pissed off, thinking Ace should have solved his problem.

"Okay, buddy, you ready?" He rolled back the little stool he was sitting on and looked at me with his goggle glasses.

"Me?" I answered, pointing to myself. "Are you kidding me?" I put the transfers on a table, my buddy did the same, and we left the shop with a string of swear words beating our backs.

Chapter 29

It felt good to be doing something creative again. I sat there for a while, lying back in the chair, thinking. I saw Marilyn drive into the garage and walk out alone. She entered the back door as I got to the kitchen with a question, "Where's Emma?"

She heard my obvious concern and saw it on my face. "Calm down, hon'. We ran into a woman who administers the group home that Emma was in when she was fifteen. A woman that Emma really likes. I suggested she take Carol, that's her name, to lunch if Carol could bring her home. So that's where she is, our little girl hobnobbing on the town." I could appreciate that. I just didn't know where Marilyn came up with words like *hobnobbing.*

I made tea, and we sat around the table with a box of Graham crackers. The cat was winding around our ankles. I told her I had called Sylvia, who was at a conference.

"I know."

"You know?" I said with raised eyebrows.

"I spoke with her last week."

"You didn't tell me that."

"I don't tell you everything. We usually speak together once a week."

I felt like my domain was being violated. "May I ask what you guys talk about?" I sounded a little snippy.

"Sure, things that a concerned mother wants to know about how her daughter is coping."

"And?"

"She's doing very well."

I decided that this conversation was going nowhere and went to my office when my phone rang. It was Dicky with my excuse. I responded loud enough for Marilyn to hear that I would be glad to help him tomorrow and would be there at about nine o'clock. "Take care, Dick; I'll see you tomorrow." I think the nervousness of my lie caused me to add, "take care."

When Carol brought her home, Emma invited her to *meet her dad.* I was so proud. And she took her upstairs to see her room. Before she left, Carol shook hands with me, then clasped her other hand on top and, beginning to tear up, she could only say, "Thank you." She did the same with Marilyn, who put on a coat and walked her to her car.

I called Dicky's cell and got the script for tomorrow's play two days before New Year's Eve.

***

This was going to be easier than I thought; both my girls were sleeping in. I showered in the downstairs bathroom and then dressed in casual clothes. I left a note saying, *Gone to Dicky's, remember. Luv you both. See ya later.* I covered one corner with a cup as though I expected it to blow away.

***

Dr. Kim's office was somewhat spartan, as though she did not value the trappings of some medical offices that had hired interior designers. However, she did have several high-quality, black-and-white framed photographs of distant landscapes that were quite beautiful. As I examined these, the receptionist said, "Doctor Kim's hobby; her husband is a photojournalist, also. He's on assignment now with *Rolling Stone* magazine in Afghanistan." I was totally impressed.

I was received and escorted to Exam Room 3 by a young Asian-American woman in a white coat with no name or title over the pocket. When she closed the door, she extended her hand and said, "I'm Doctor Kim, Mr. Phillips. What seems to be the problem?"

I didn't answer right away. At first, I was surprised this was the doctor, and then a little pissed off by the word "seems."

She weighed me, then patted the paper-covered exam table. As I hoisted myself onto it, she pulled on latex gloves. "My problem is in my stomach, right about here." I pointed to the location. That was all I could manage.

"Please unbutton your shirt, open your belt and zipper, and lie back." Then she added, "Relax, Mr. Phillips, this is a minimal examination. There'll be no penetration." I don't know why I laughed; probably nervousness, but when she laughed, I began to relax.

As she pushed here and there and stethoscoped me, I looked at the framed documents on the wall. I was reassured by the diplomas and certificates from quality universities and several hospitals. Then, she pressed harder midway down my abdomen, and I yelped.

She did it again, saying, "Quite sensitive there?" I managed a weak *yes* through clenched teeth.

"Okay, sit up and face that way." She indicated the picture wall, then came behind me, clenching her hands around my stomach. "This may tingle a little," she said while pulling back and up like a Heimlich maneuver. I thought I would pass out. "You can fix your clothes now."

She was typing notes into a tablet on the counter near the scale. I was still sitting on the table, trying to read both the notes and her mind.

She turned to me, indicating a chair, and said, "You can sit there."

She sat on a padded, wheeled stool and brought it closer to me, leaning forward to reassure me. "I'm going to set up a few tests for you. I will order this for Friday. Unless you hear differently, you must report to Ambulatory Care at ten a.m. Do not eat or drink anything after ten p.m. tomorrow night."

I don't know why, but all I could think about was how hungry I would be on New Year's Eve.

"Do you have any questions?"

"Of course I do," I answered a little too sharply. "What is it?"

She wheeled a little closer, and I could see this was not an answer she wanted to give. "Obviously, I need to see all the test results, Mr. Phillips, But I'm not going to kid you. I think that would be cruel. I think you have a mass, probably on your liver." She reached out and clasped my hand, and the expression on her face was of someone who really cared. I felt better about her now.

Trying to lessen my fear, she described the possible protocols that could significantly impact my treatment program. "And new treatments are coming out every day." She finished by saying there is a lot of hope today and directed me to weigh myself each morning and keep a log. A follow-up appointment was scheduled for Monday. All test results would be available by then. Monday, Jan. 5. She had the wisdom not to wish me a *Happy New Year*. Now, I needed to get past Marilyn.

***

There must be some divine intervention going on. When I got home from my appointment, Emma was in the kitchen, wearing one of Marilyn's aprons, with a table full of ingredients, preparing to bake a pie. The flour smudge on her cheek was adorable. She was in a jubilant mood. "Guess what I'm doing, Dad?"

"Um… getting ready to shampoo the cat."

"Nooo… I'm making a pecan pie. Mom says it's your favorite."

"It is. Oh, man, that'll be great. Do we have whipped cream?"

She looked at me as if I'd grown another nose. "Of course, we got all that stuff this morning when we went shopping."

Marilyn heard us talking and came into the room, putting her arms around me from the back to kiss my neck. My first impulse was to stiffen up, ready for the pain that Dr. Kim had probed.

"Hey, loosen up," she said, resting her head on my back. "You're really tight; sit down." So, I sat, and she massaged my shoulders while Emma kept mixing and humming some popular tune. I could tell they had something going on.

Finally, Emma teased, "Guess where we're going Friday."

"To feed the ducks at the zoo pond?"

"Nooo…" she whisked a little flour in my direction. "Mom's taking me to a spa." Then she exploded in giggles. "I can't wait, I can't wait, I can't wait."

"When do you do this?"

Marilyn jumped in, "Friday, we have to be there by nine thirty, and with lunch, we won't be back until at least two. Will you be able to manage by yourself?"

I nodded, tilted my head back, closed my eyes, and said to myself, *Thank you, Jesus.*

***

I called Dicky to thank him again and tell him about my office visit and the Friday tests. Then, he asked, "Do you want me to drive you?"

I declined, saying, "Nah, been there, done that with Charlie." When I said that, I suddenly realized that I probably had cancer, *the big C*, I started to shake. I heard the girls laughing in the kitchen, full-on into pie baking. I thought, *Please don't let them come here now.* That sounded like a prayer to me.

I got out of my chair, slipped into the entry hall, got a heavy coat and hat from the closet, and quietly went outside.

It was snowing; light, fluffy flakes that were whisked away by my feet. I wasn't sure how far I walked. But by the time I returned, my shoes were making inch-deep tracks. I planned to slip back in the front door, but it was locked, and I had no key.

I startled the girls when I entered the back door; they were unaware I had left. Marilyn grabbed a wooden spoon, holding it like a weapon. "Jesus, Dex, you scared us. I thought it was some sort of maniacal, serial killer, sex pervert."

"What makes you think it isn't?"

"You don't have that much energy." She grinned, putting down the weapon. Emma was laughing herself into tears.

***

While walking, I thought about Charlie and how he'd handled it. I also thought maybe it wasn't cancer, but I was only kidding myself, like most afflicted people grasping at straws.

Assuming the worst, I began to think about all I had to do, and the first thing that came to mind was getting a will. I had never thought about it before, and that was stupid. I had a family now. I'd call Marty first thing Monday morning. The next thing that came to mind was how I would handle this? I doubted I had the courage of Charlie, who had accepted his fate and said, "Fuck it, bring it on," and willed himself to die.

***

New Year's Eve — why bother? This was never much of a holiday in our family and when I met Marilyn, I was glad she felt the same way. Emma said she had too many bad memories and asked if we could just hang out, have popcorn and pecan pie with lots of whipped cream, and listen to music. It was evident we were a family now.

***

I went through the series of tests. The girls survived the spa day. We got on with the new year.

What little snow we had gotten melted in the driveway in front of the garage. I decided to show Emma how to shoot baskets.

She got a kick out of it and did quite well. She was using a two-hand push shot from the line, sinking four out of ten, and was very proud of herself. Marilyn called from the door that the hot chocolate was ready. Father and daughter walked to the house, arm in arm, red-faced, noses dripping from the cold. I managed to dribble the ball up the stairs with my left hand.

Our Sunday routine now consisted of an Emma-made breakfast, the paper, and *Meet the Press*, for which Emma had to write a report for school. This Sunday, we spent time talking about school. Marilyn had scheduled an appointment with the community college admissions counselor for Tuesday; classes started in two weeks. Everything was moving ahead rapidly. We were all running out of time. Emma only had another week of courses at Meadowbrook, several counseling sessions with Sylvia, and a cottage "Graduation" with her mates.

Chapter 30

As directed by Dr. Kim, I weighed myself that morning and was a pound lighter than in her office, but that could have been a difference in scales.

The first call I got Monday morning was from a guy trying to sell me a home security system. I sat there holding the dead phone in my hand; the last thing I needed was a telemarketing call. By ten, I'd heard nothing. So what the hell were they waiting for?

Phone again: *TOM B.*

"Hey, Dex, Happy New Year."

"Thanks, same to you." I thought about telling him about my potential medical problem but decided to wait for the test results.

"Hey, I've got something that could be good for Emma. Tom Farrell at Vantage Financial said he could use a part-time intern around the office. He's on the top floor of my building. They handle all my stuff. They're a good outfit."

"Intern, as in no pay?"

"Hell no, I told him he needed to come up with a pretty good figure, or I might have to move some of my stuff to another broker."

"I should have known, T. You're the best. So, what's our next move?" I was beginning to feel good all over.

"Have Emma call Mrs. Winifred Prescott, Farrell's executive assistant, for an appointment. I've gotta go; we're going down to Mary Ellen's place for a few days. I'll call you when I return. Everything good with you?"

"Terrific." Yes, I did feel good about this opportunity for Emma.

The next call was from Dr. Kim. She gave it to me without a sugarcoat. "There is a mass. It is certainly malignant. Tomorrow, ten a.m., Southside East. I'm sorry."

I felt like shit — and scared shitless.

***

If I'd had a bullet to bite, I could use it now. But how could I break this to my family? I ran through several scenarios in my overactive imagination; none were satisfactory. So, finally, I decided to keep the truth to myself and work on my lying skills a little longer. The girls were enjoying this time of no commitment by sleeping in. So, I figured I could get to the hospital at eight, submit to whatever they had planned for me, and be back home by ten when sleepy heads were not too sharp, and I could bullshit my way clear.

Emma made her interview appointment at Vantage Financial, and Marilyn immediately began thinking of a professional wardrobe for her. Marilyn again mentioned the Tuesday appointment with the college admissions counselor. When I heard her repeat the day and time, I wanted to jump up and shout. Fortunately, I had dodged another one.

They would be leaving the house by nine. I tried to sound appropriately disappointed when I said, "You guys should go alone. You don't need me butting in; it's Emma's show." I was a little surprised and disappointed when Mar agreed so quickly, as if I really would be in the way,

As much as I was relieved by this, I began to see it as a long downward spiral. I was lying out of a situation I wanted to be part of. And I realized that, soon enough, I might be physically unable to participate. It was a shitty, hollow feeling, and I felt nauseous. At this early stage, I wasn't sure if I was nauseous because of the way I felt or the disease.

***

They wanted to put a port in me, like a straw in a juice box, so subsequent chemo treatments could be more easily administered. I refused. They tried to explain more, but I declined more. I had Charlie in my corner.

Taking his advice, I had the foot massage while I lay back in the recliner, facing up to the wall-mounted TV, quietly babbling on about stupid shit. The massage woman was nice enough to not attempt conversation.

I felt alright when they finished, and they gave me a glass of orange juice and a pep talk. When I reached my car, I opened the door and vomited before I got in. Splashing some bilious-looking liquid on my shoes. I felt better after that, but unlike Charlie, I had no desire to get a drink. I went home and went to bed.

Two hours later, I heard the excited voices below and then Emma and the cat racing up the stairs. I'm sure she wondered about the closed door, but I occasionally took naps. I imagined she changed from *Miss College Student Admittee* into jeans and a sweatshirt. I'd get up after she goes downstairs and check myself out.

I came down all casual and smiling, hugged her, and asked, "Well, how'd it go?" As if the glow on her face didn't tell me.

"*Awwsuum*, I'm so stoked, I could puke." I had to laugh at her convoluted metaphor.

"Tell me all about it."

She dragged me into the living room, sat on the couch, and excitedly told me about the college. And also had visual aids in the form of brochures, syllabi, notebooks, textbooks, a backpack, a Marlborough Mustangs sweatshirt, and team sports schedules. But she was most proud of the Jane Austen novel, her namesake.

She did a lot of excited talking with her hands. Marilyn was standing in the doorway, looking like one of the saints. I tried hard not to show the pain racking my guts.

The next excitement was when Emma was hired by Tom Farrell. He probably would not have hired her if he had seen how giddy she was when she returned home. She was running on some sugar high of positive emotions and couldn't sit still or shut up. I struggled to keep up with her enthusiasm but thought I had covered my tracks well.

That night when we went to bed, Marilyn got up on one elbow and got right in my face. "What's going on?"

I tried to play the "what" card. "What do you mean?"

She was having none of it. "Do *not* bullshit me!" I knew she meant it. "Why do you weigh yourself every morning?"

Shit, I left the list in the bathroom. "Hey, just trying to stay healthy."

"Healthy is losing five pounds in six days? You're a *fucking* liar!" She hit me with those words as if they were her fists.

"I'm sick, Mar. I've been sick for a while."

She didn't move; her mouth was open but with no sound. Then, finally, she started to tear up. And then, a cry of utter despair. Finally, she shut off a grotesque wailing sound by burying her head in my chest. Her shoulders were heaving as she cried and rattled, soaking my pajama top.

Her body pinned my left arm to the bed while I stroked her hair with my right hand and rubbed her back, softly saying things that didn't make any sense. We lay that way for a while. Even when she stopped crying, she clung to me as if I might be taken away. "Mar… Mar… we've got to talk about this. Can we do that, Mar… we need to talk." Finally, she raised her head and nodded, then scrambled from the bed and just made it to the bathroom before she started retching.

***

We sat there in silence for what seemed like hours, but it was only a few minutes. I offered to get tea, and Marilyn asked in a little girl's voice if I would make hot chocolate. She was devastated and could not move. I took her hand and kissed it. As I walked by Emma's door, I kissed my fingers and pressed them to the wood.

I returned with a filled thermos, two mugs, and a can of whipped cream. I poured it into her mug and gave it a shot of the cream. She asked for more. She took a sip and looked like a *Got Milk?* commercial with a whipped cream mustache. I kissed it away as she stuck her tongue out a little.

Our conversation began naturally enough. We started reminiscing, going over the good times. Marilyn chuckled when she remembered gunning the basketball at my crotch, "God, I was pissed at you." She said, now smiling.

We talked about trips, and when we rented a small sailboat and tipped it over. Getting the cat from the humane shelter and getting the flu. We covered all the bases of our three-year relationship, soon to be four years. We had both lost mates before. We knew where we were headed.

We talked about Emma. There was no doubt from either of us that a mother/daughter relationship would be maintained and strengthened. I told her about Marty and the will that was drawn up. It was simple enough. The house would be in Marilyn's name with the condition that it would go to Emma upon her passing. Our checking and savings accounts were in both names, so that was no problem. An investment account that I had alone would now be in her name. And a separate trust fund was set up to ensure Emma's future.

We talked about death. I had always tried to push Barbara's death out of my mind. But now, thirty-odd years later, it seemed like yesterday. I guess my own condition brought it back into focus. I thought of Barbara in the treatment protocols of that time and how day by day, hope rose and fell like an ocean tide. I saw pieces and flakes of her life drop away like autumn leaves as she fought a losing battle. I was determined not to do that. I would do it in one big chunk.

I did not want Emma to know I was sick. "Please, Mar, I never want her to know."

"Of course, she'll know, Dex; you can't hide it forever."

I turned and looked at her, "It won't be forever."

***

We lay there holding hands, and as we did so often, she fell asleep. I wasn't sure if I ever did, and I finally got up in the dark at 6:15. I put the coffee on and went to my office, intending to do something, but I wasn't sure what. I needed to look ahead. I needed to get going on the book. So, I booted up my laptop. I felt like "booting" it out in the snow this morning.

I still had twenty four hand-written "narratives" to transcribe, which was a laborious task since I had never learned to type correctly in all these years. So, I thought of myself as a chicken, hunting and pecking for cracked corn — twenty-four pieces at three pieces a day; eight days.

After my second cup, I decided to call Tom. I knew it would go to voicemail, but the first thing he did on his mid-morning wake-up was to check for messages. I kept it brief, "I'll buy you a cheap lunch at the alleys, and if you don't piss me off, maybe a beer. Call me when your lazy ass is finally out of bed." I hated to do this, but he had to know before the league started tonight.

***

The first clue for him was the booth. In the same way that Dicky knew, Tom suspected something.

When I finished, he covered his face with his hands and sat like that for a minute, knowing words wouldn't help. Finally, he got up, reached over, squeezed my shoulder with a grip showing concern, put on his coat, said, "See you tonight," and left. I raised my nearly empty bottle and signaled for another beer.

Earlier that morning, I had been sitting at the kitchen table with the cat curled in my lap. Marilyn came in, hugged and kissed me, and asked if I wanted another cup. We were playing our parts correctly because when Emma appeared, dressed for work and bursting with promise, she didn't suspect anything. She took the cat from my lap, kissed my cheek, and then went to her mother.

"I'm stoked, Mom, my first day at work." She said that with a rising inflection as she shifted the cat under her arm and poured a cup of coffee. She was dressed in "office" clothes because Mrs. Prescott had called yesterday and asked if Emma could come in for a few hours. "Can I use your car, Dad? It's a power color."

I had to laugh at that, "Sure."

***

That night, we lost three out of four matches and ended in sixth place at the start of the league. Tom's cousin, Russell, Charlie's replacement, rolled best. I wondered who would replace me.

***

I kept up a pretty good pace of editing and transcribing my narratives. But, keeping to my three-a-day goal, I could feel the tiredness increasing as much as my weight loss. I had dropped twelve pounds since my first day with Dr. Kim not that long ago. My clothes had begun to hang.

I set up an outline for the complete story, arranging the chapters as I thought best. All it needed was the connective tissue, and it would be finished. Anyone can do that.

Wednesday night, I gave it my best shot, but rolled a gutter ball in the last frame.

Epilogue

It was a perfect day for outdoor graduation exercises and achievement award presentations at Marlborough Community College. Warmer than usual for early June, with a cloudless sky and a light southwest breeze. The stage was set in front of the field house and decorated in maroon and white bunting, the college team colors. The eager graduates were seated in the first two rows, splendid in their caps and gowns. On stage behind the podium, the achievement award recipients were seated with Emma on the far right. She was beautiful in a light gray pantsuit with a colorful scarf draped from her shoulders. Her hair was drawn back in a French Twist that gave her a sophisticated look beyond her nineteen years. Marilyn was seated in the fifth row behind the graduates clutching a tissue in her hands for the joyful tears that would follow. Newly-married Tom and Mary Ellen Brandt were beside her.

Dr. Georgina Cromwell, President of the College, welcomed the graduates, guests, and speakers with a brief speech about the role and traditions of the school. Then, Dean Harold Nardone came to the podium to announce the achievement awards. Next, Emma Phillips was presented with the award for Literary Achievement and went to the podium to address the assembly.

"My name is Emma Phillips. I have recently completed a novel started by my father, Dexter Phillips, nearly a year ago. He was so close to finishing when he died in a single-car accident returning home from the bowling league. Bowling was only one of his passions. He also loved to shoot hoops in the backyard. Dad spent many hours framing this book. He loved the companionship of his lifelong friends. His greatest passion was his family.

"My father, Dexter Phillips, rescued me. I was not born into this family. I came into it through his goodness and generosity. I assumed the daughter role and was accepted by him and his life partner, Marilyn Brewer. I call her *Mom*, and we will carry on the family.

Dad had carefully laid out the skeleton of his book. All the bones were arranged correctly on his computer. So all I had to do was flesh it out.

As a student here at Marlborough, I had the opportunity to work with Professor Angela Stewart, who guided me through this process. Her assistance and the facilities available to me here at the college allowed the publication of this book funded by a foundation set up by my mom, the Phillips Educational Trust. Dad taught me how to live confidently and guided me through difficult times. It is in his honor that I finished his work, *Dexter Phillips' First Novel,* and dedicate this award to him."

Emma raised the award plaque and looked to the heavens as the assembly clapped and cheered.

Marilyn brought the tissue to her eyes, looked up, and softly said in a strained voice, "Good on ya, Dex. I'll always love you. Take care."

END